STONE ARCH BOOKS
a capstone imprint

STONE ARCH BOOKS™

Published in 2013
A Capstone Imprint
1710 Roe Crest Drive
North Mankato, MN 56003
www.capstonepub.com

Originally published by DC Comics in the U.S. in single
magazine form as Batman Adventures #6.

DC Comics
1700 Broadway, New York, NY 10019
A Warner Bros. Entertainment Company

Printed in China by Nordica.
0413/CA21300442
032013 007226NORDF13

Cataloging-in-Publication Data is available at the Library of Congress website:
ISBN: 978-1-4342-6034-5 (library binding)

Summary: Batman's out to bust the various rackets of the gangster named Black Mask, but he's playing with fire when he goes after the Mask's pet arsonist: Firefly!

STONE ARCH BOOKS

Ashley C. Andersen Zantop *Publisher*
Michael Dahl *Editorial Director*
Donald Lemke & Sean Tulien *Editors*
Heather Kindseth *Creative Director*
Bob Lentz & Alison Thiele *Designers*
Kathy McColley *Production Specialist*

DC COMICS

Joan Hilty *Original U.S. Editor*
Harvey Richards *U.S. Assistant Editor*
Kelsey Shannon *Cover Artist*

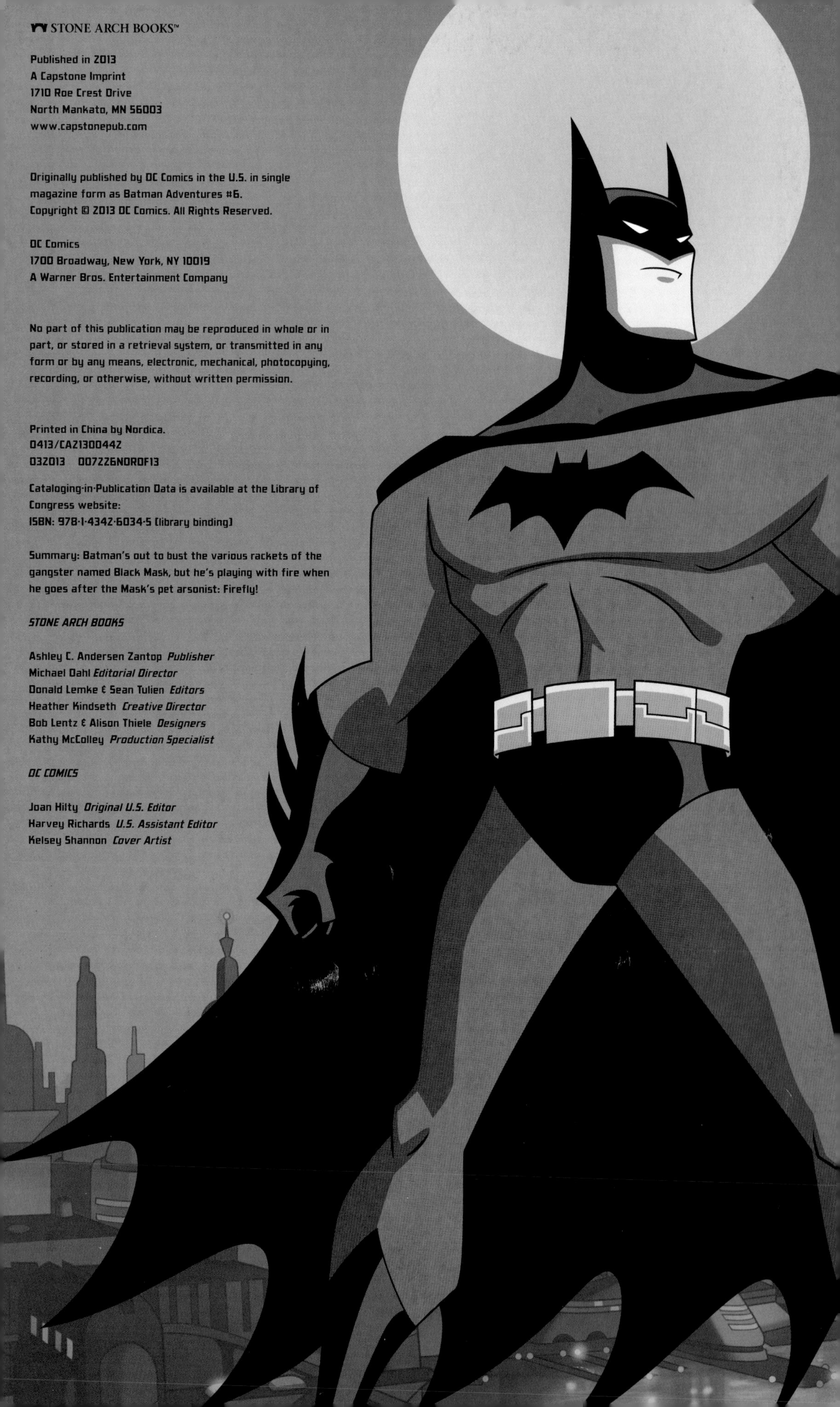

BATMAN ADVENTURES

PLAYING WITH MATCHES

Dan Slott ....writer
Rick Burchett ....penciller
Terry Beatty..inker
Lee Loughridge ....colorist
Rob Leigh...letterer

**Batman created by
Bob Kane**

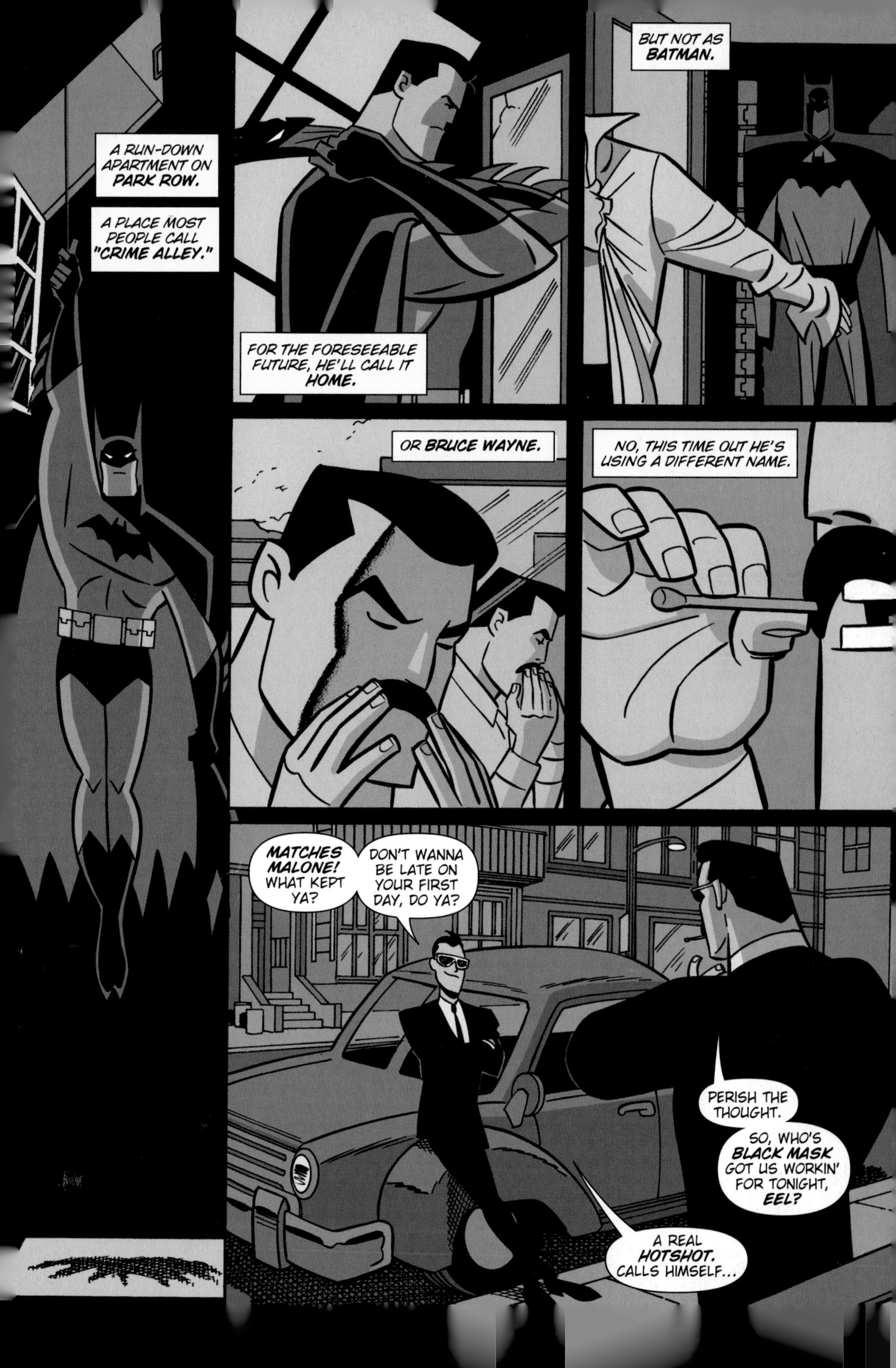
A RUN-DOWN APARTMENT ON PARK ROW.
A PLACE MOST PEOPLE CALL "CRIME ALLEY."
FOR THE FORESEEABLE FUTURE, HE'LL CALL IT HOME.
BUT NOT AS BATMAN.
OR BRUCE WAYNE.
NO, THIS TIME OUT HE'S USING A DIFFERENT NAME.
MATCHES MALONE! WHAT KEPT YA?
DON'T WANNA BE LATE ON YOUR FIRST DAY, DO YA?
PERISH THE THOUGHT.
SO, WHO'S BLACK MASK GOT US WORKIN' FOR TONIGHT, EEL?
A REAL HOTSHOT. CALLS HIMSELF...

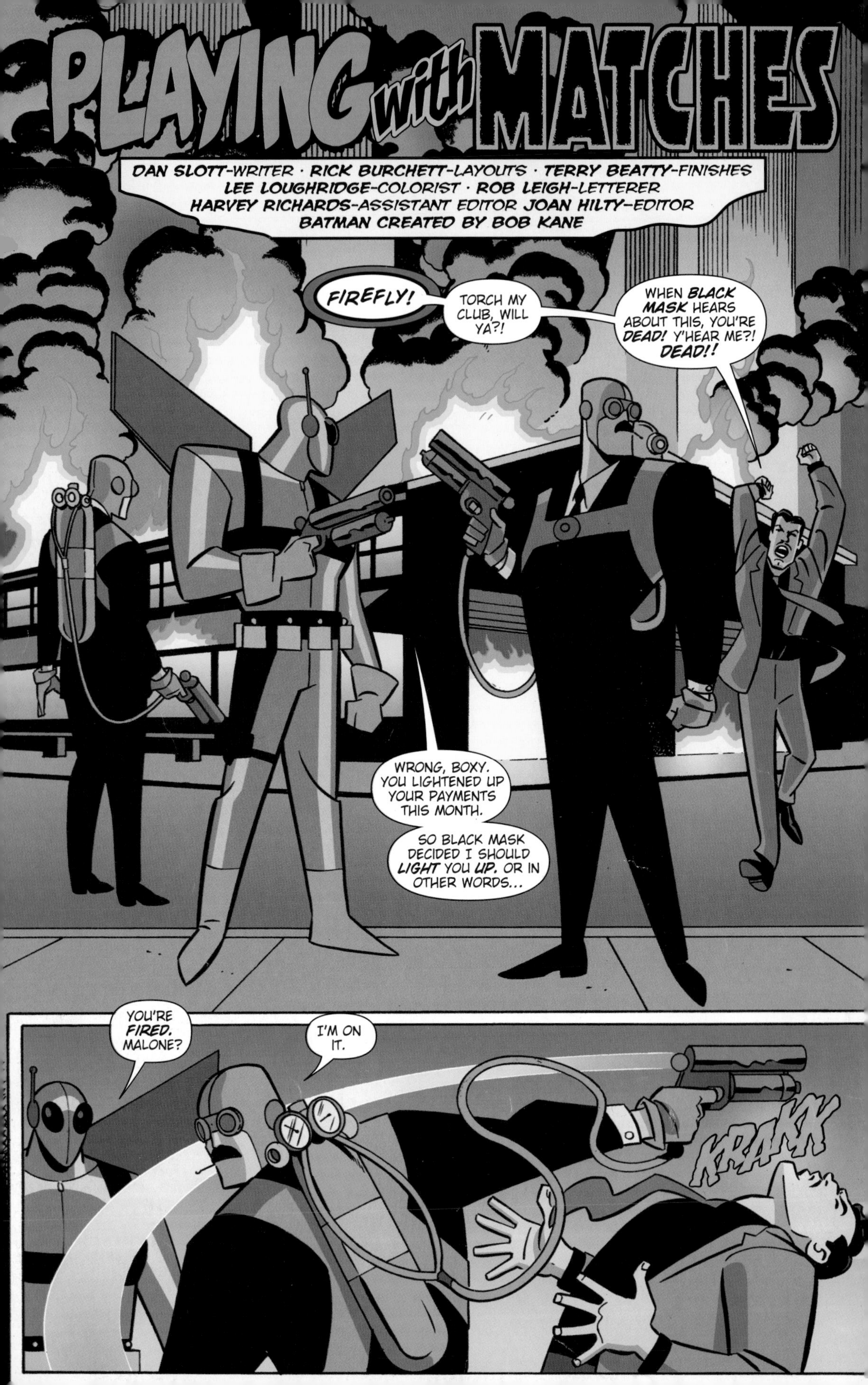
PLAYING with MATCHES
DAN SLOTT-WRITER · RICK BURCHETT-LAYOUTS · TERRY BEATTY-FINISHES
LEE LOUGHRIDGE-COLORIST · ROB LEIGH-LETTERER
HARVEY RICHARDS-ASSISTANT EDITOR JOAN HILTY-EDITOR
BATMAN CREATED BY BOB KANE
FIREFLY!
TORCH MY CLUB, WILL YA?!
WHEN BLACK MASK HEARS ABOUT THIS, YOU'RE DEAD! Y'HEAR ME?! DEAD!!
WRONG, BOXY. YOU LIGHTENED UP YOUR PAYMENTS THIS MONTH.
SO BLACK MASK DECIDED I SHOULD LIGHT YOU UP. OR IN OTHER WORDS...
YOU'RE FIRED. MALONE?
I'M ON IT.
KRAKK

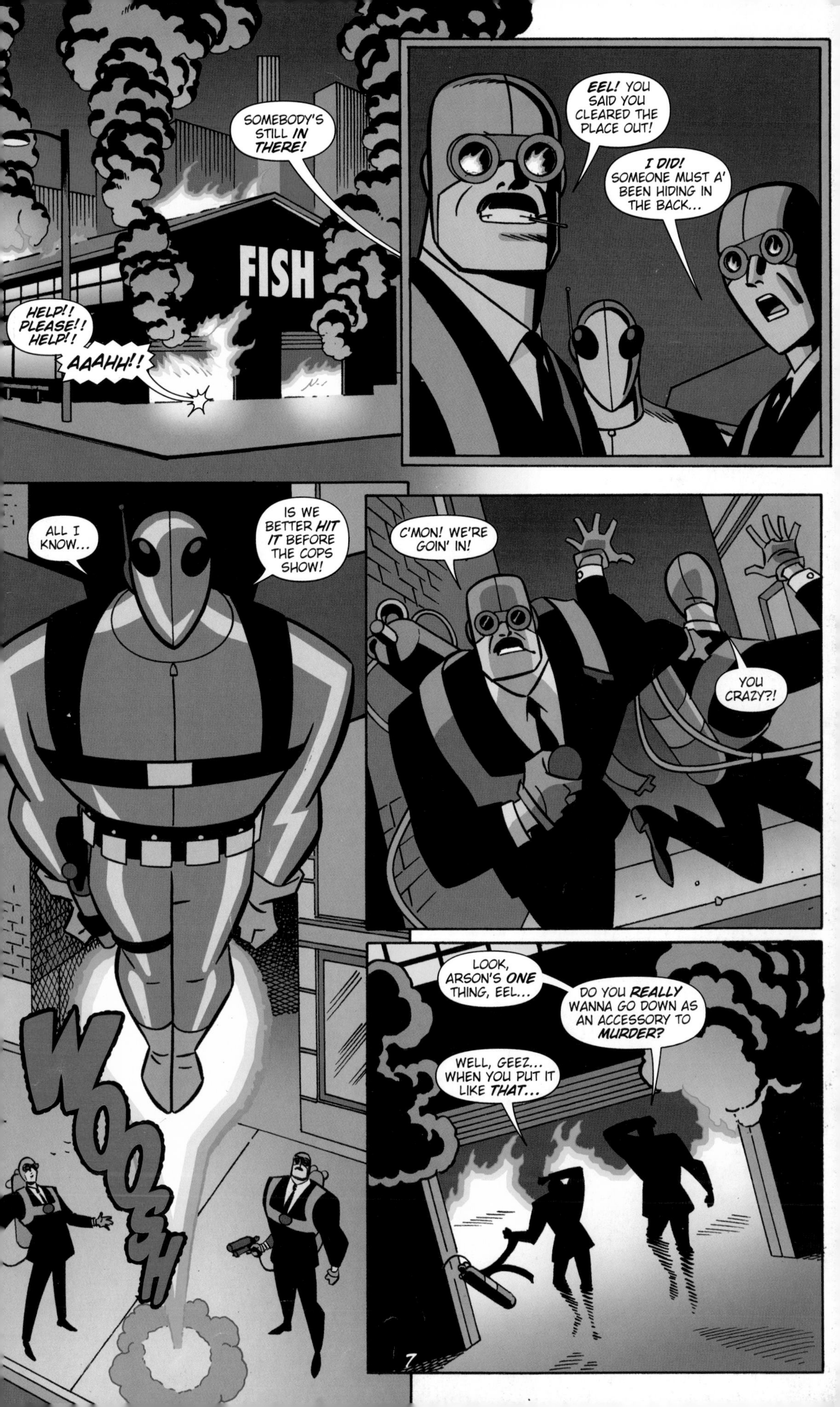

SOMEBODY'S STILL IN THERE!
FISH
HELP!! PLEASE!! HELP!!
AAAHH!!
EEL! YOU SAID YOU CLEARED THE PLACE OUT!
I DID! SOMEONE MUST A' BEEN HIDING IN THE BACK...
ALL I KNOW...
IS WE BETTER HIT IT BEFORE THE COPS SHOW!
WOOSH
C'MON! WE'RE GOIN' IN!
YOU CRAZY?!
LOOK, ARSON'S ONE THING, EEL...
DO YOU REALLY WANNA GO DOWN AS AN ACCESSORY TO MURDER?
WELL, GEEZ... WHEN YOU PUT IT LIKE THAT...

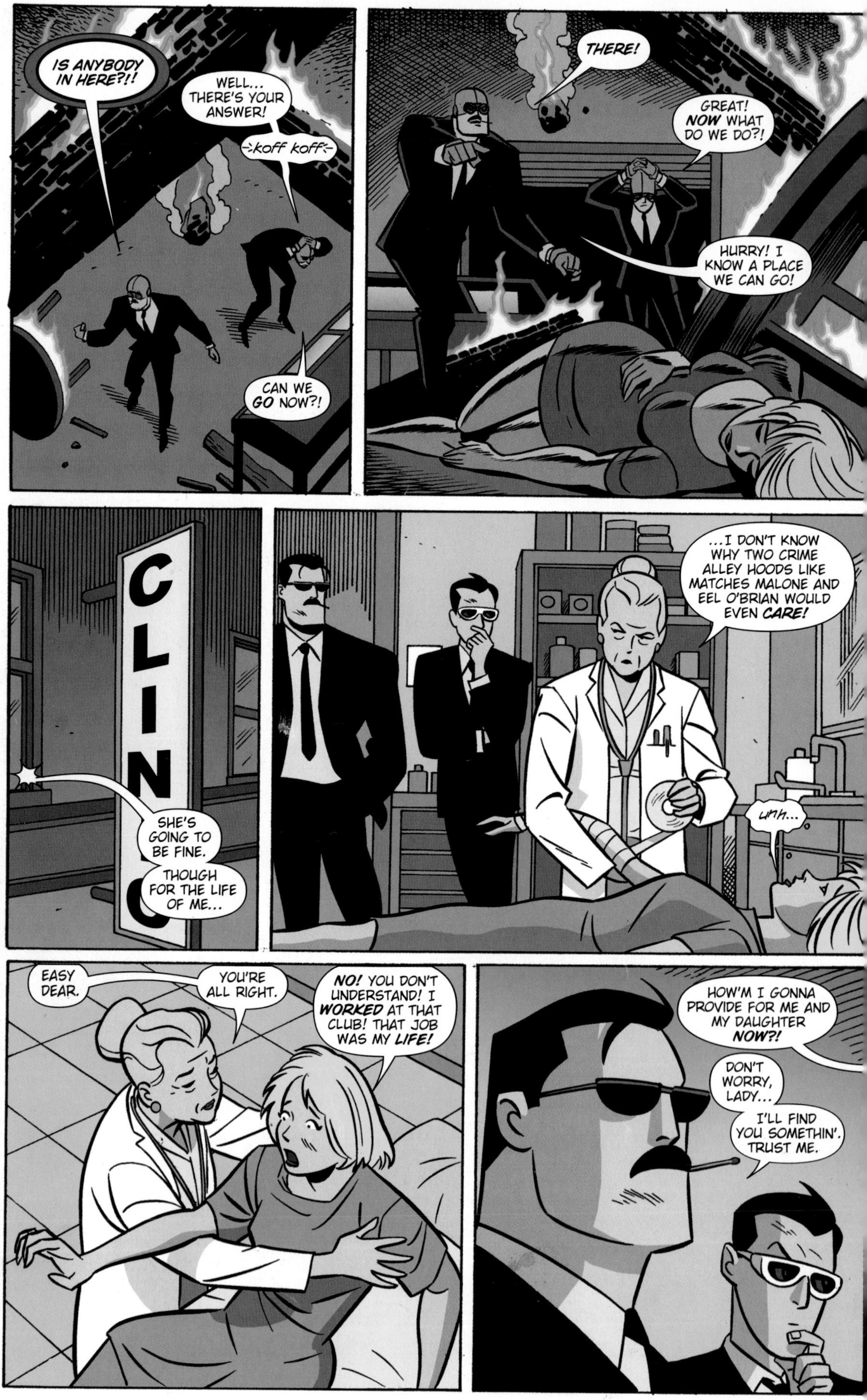
IS ANYBODY IN HERE?!!
WELL... THERE'S YOUR ANSWER!
koff koff
CAN WE GO NOW?!
THERE!
GREAT! NOW WHAT DO WE DO?!
HURRY! I KNOW A PLACE WE CAN GO!
CLINIC
SHE'S GOING TO BE FINE.
THOUGH FOR THE LIFE OF ME...
...I DON'T KNOW WHY TWO CRIME ALLEY HOODS LIKE MATCHES MALONE AND EEL O'BRIAN WOULD EVEN CARE!
unh...
EASY DEAR.
YOU'RE ALL RIGHT.
NO! YOU DON'T UNDERSTAND! I WORKED AT THAT CLUB! THAT JOB WAS MY LIFE!
HOW'M I GONNA PROVIDE FOR ME AND MY DAUGHTER NOW?!
DON'T WORRY, LADY...
I'LL FIND YOU SOMETHIN'. TRUST ME.

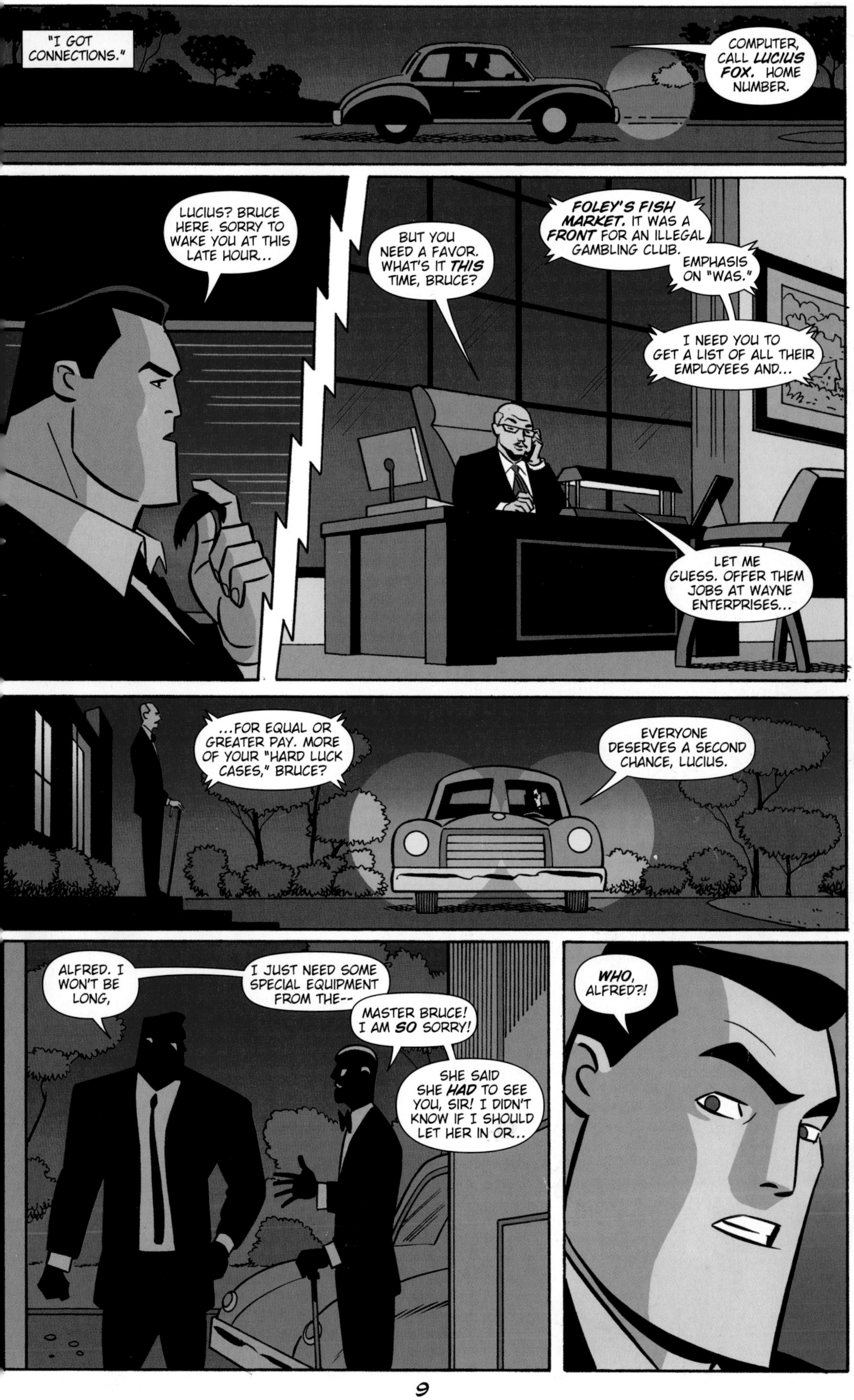
"I GOT CONNECTIONS."
COMPUTER, CALL LUCIUS FOX. HOME NUMBER.
LUCIUS? BRUCE HERE. SORRY TO WAKE YOU AT THIS LATE HOUR...
BUT YOU NEED A FAVOR. WHAT'S IT THIS TIME, BRUCE?
FOLEY'S FISH MARKET. IT WAS A FRONT FOR AN ILLEGAL GAMBLING CLUB.
EMPHASIS ON "WAS."
I NEED YOU TO GET A LIST OF ALL THEIR EMPLOYEES AND...
LET ME GUESS. OFFER THEM JOBS AT WAYNE ENTERPRISES...
...FOR EQUAL OR GREATER PAY. MORE OF YOUR "HARD LUCK CASES," BRUCE?
EVERYONE DESERVES A SECOND CHANCE, LUCIUS.
ALFRED. I WON'T BE LONG,
I JUST NEED SOME SPECIAL EQUIPMENT FROM THE--
MASTER BRUCE! I AM SO SORRY!
SHE SAID SHE HAD TO SEE YOU, SIR! I DIDN'T KNOW IF I SHOULD LET HER IN OR...
WHO, ALFRED?!

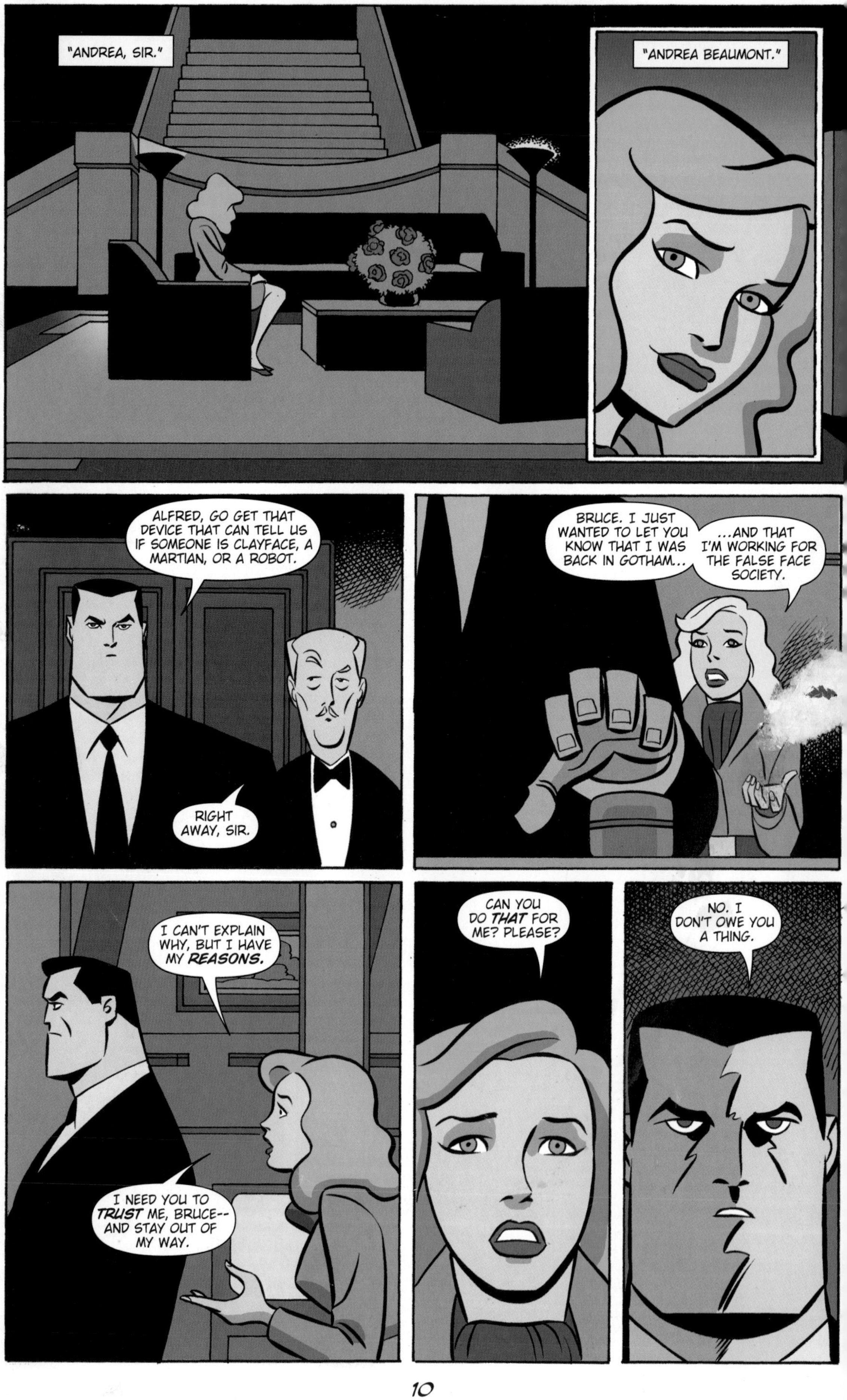
"ANDREA, SIR."
"ANDREA BEAUMONT."
ALFRED, GO GET THAT DEVICE THAT CAN TELL US IF SOMEONE IS CLAYFACE, A MARTIAN, OR A ROBOT.
RIGHT AWAY, SIR.
BRUCE. I JUST WANTED TO LET YOU KNOW THAT I WAS BACK IN GOTHAM...
...AND THAT I'M WORKING FOR THE FALSE FACE SOCIETY.
I CAN'T EXPLAIN WHY, BUT I HAVE MY *REASONS.*
I NEED YOU TO *TRUST* ME, BRUCE-- AND STAY OUT OF MY WAY.
CAN YOU DO *THAT* FOR ME? PLEASE?
NO. I DON'T OWE YOU A THING.

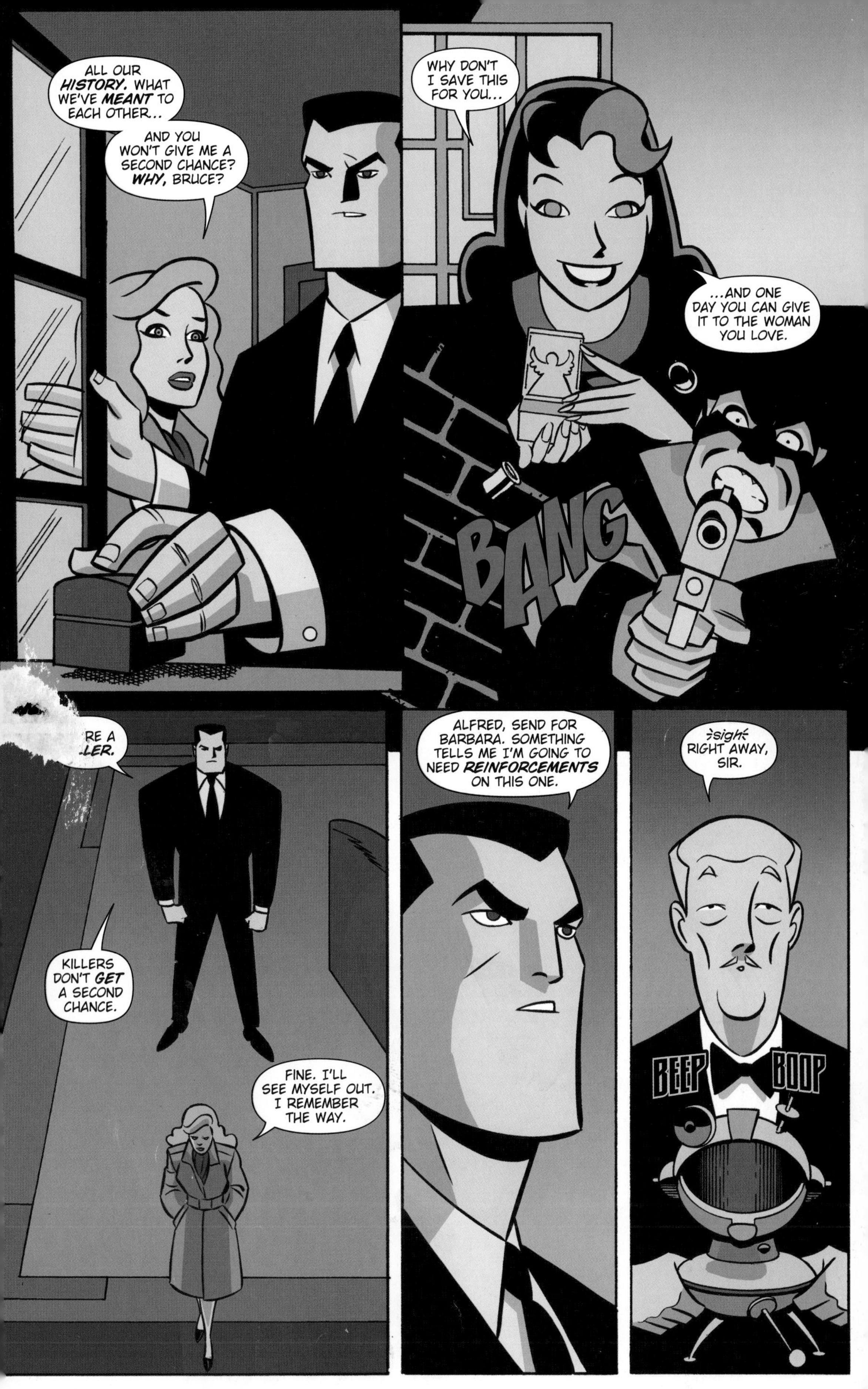
ALL OUR HISTORY. WHAT WE'VE MEANT TO EACH OTHER...
AND YOU WON'T GIVE ME A SECOND CHANCE? WHY, BRUCE?
WHY DON'T I SAVE THIS FOR YOU...
...AND ONE DAY YOU CAN GIVE IT TO THE WOMAN YOU LOVE.
BANG
RE A
LER.
KILLERS DON'T GET A SECOND CHANCE.
FINE. I'LL SEE MYSELF OUT. I REMEMBER THE WAY.
ALFRED, SEND FOR BARBARA. SOMETHING TELLS ME I'M GOING TO NEED REINFORCEMENTS ON THIS ONE.
sigh
RIGHT AWAY, SIR.
BEEP
BOOP

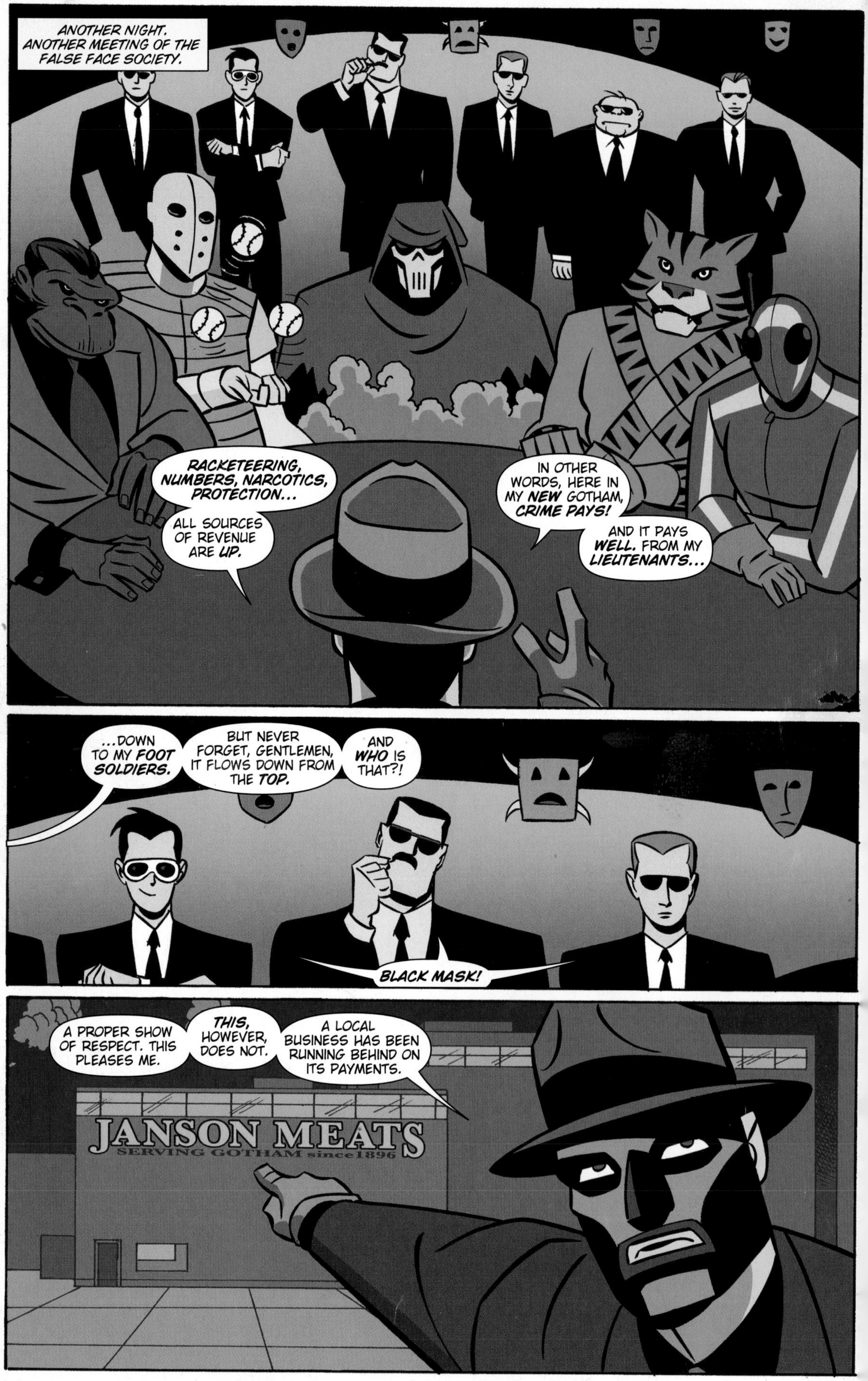
ANOTHER NIGHT. ANOTHER MEETING OF THE FALSE FACE SOCIETY.
RACKETEERING, NUMBERS, NARCOTICS, PROTECTION...
ALL SOURCES OF REVENUE ARE UP.
IN OTHER WORDS, HERE IN MY NEW GOTHAM, CRIME PAYS!
AND IT PAYS WELL. FROM MY LIEUTENANTS...
...DOWN TO MY FOOT SOLDIERS.
BUT NEVER FORGET, GENTLEMEN, IT FLOWS DOWN FROM THE TOP.
AND WHO IS THAT?!
BLACK MASK!
A PROPER SHOW OF RESPECT. THIS PLEASES ME.
THIS, HOWEVER, DOES NOT.
A LOCAL BUSINESS HAS BEEN RUNNING BEHIND ON ITS PAYMENTS.
JANSON MEATS
SERVING GOTHAM since1896

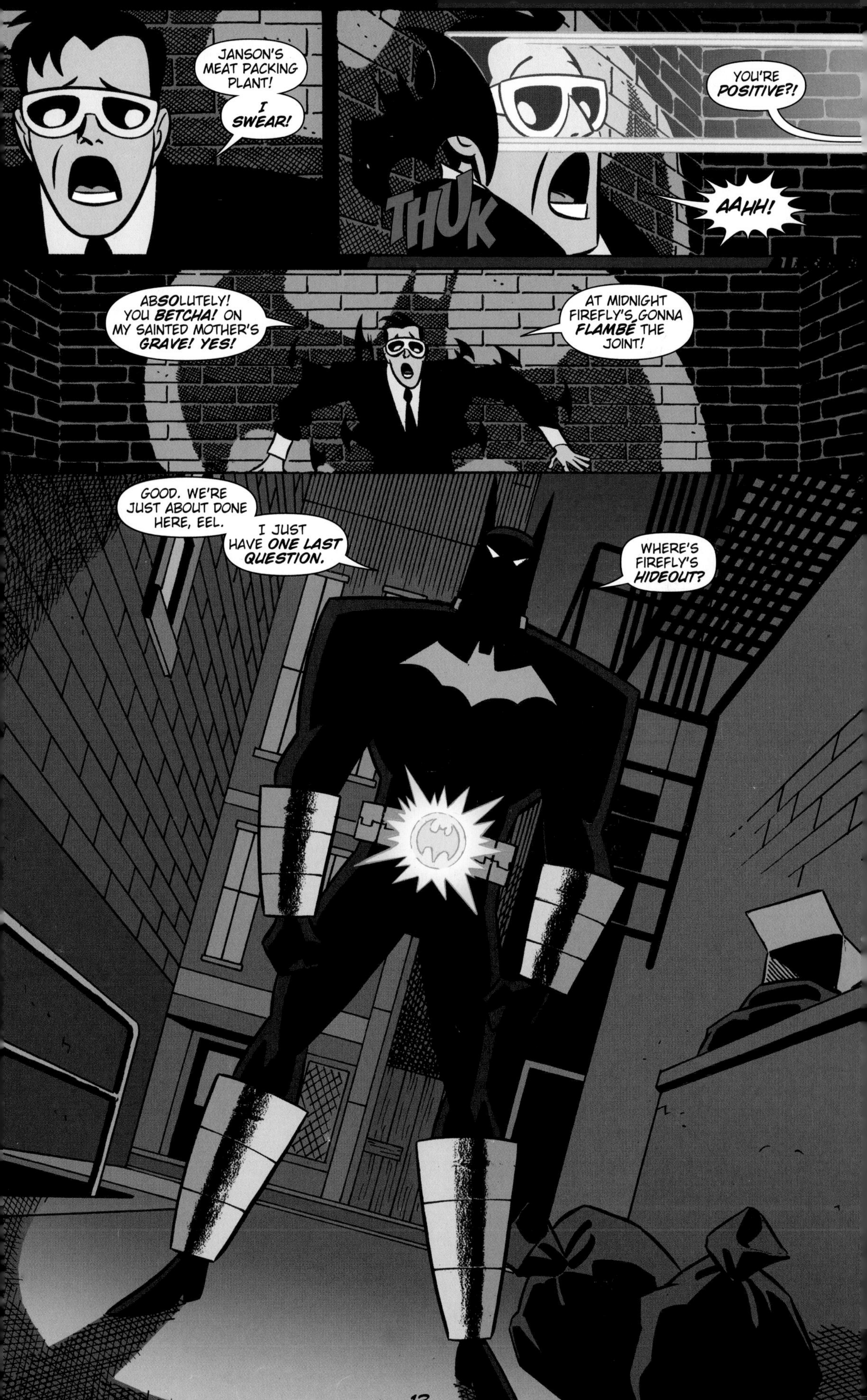
JANSON'S MEAT PACKING PLANT!
I SWEAR!
YOU'RE POSITIVE?!
THUK
AAHH!
ABSOLUTELY! YOU BETCHA! ON MY SAINTED MOTHER'S GRAVE! YES!
AT MIDNIGHT FIREFLY'S GONNA FLAMBÉ THE JOINT!
GOOD. WE'RE JUST ABOUT DONE HERE, EEL.
I JUST HAVE ONE LAST QUESTION.
WHERE'S FIREFLY'S HIDEOUT?

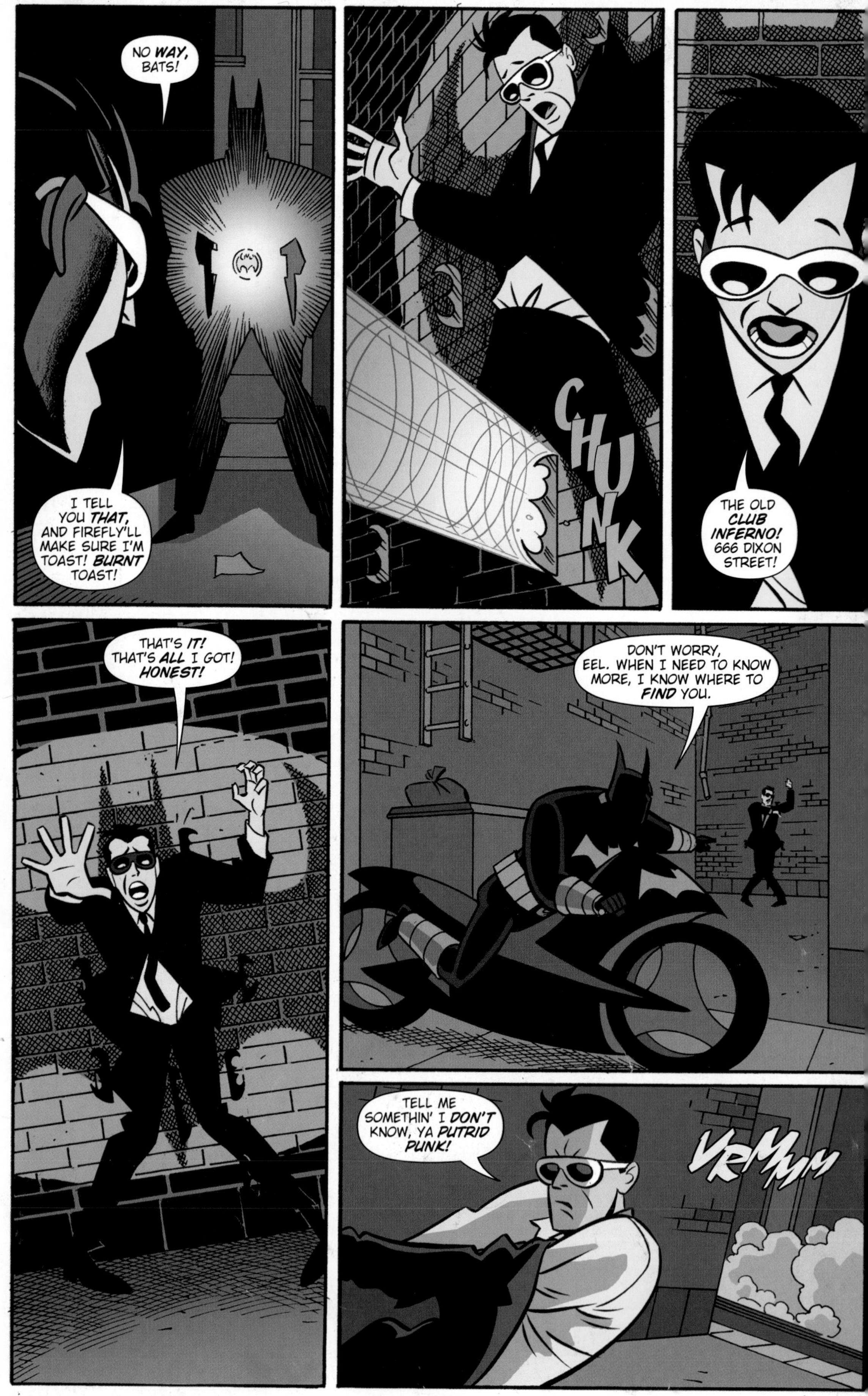
NO WAY, BATS!
I TELL YOU THAT, AND FIREFLY'LL MAKE SURE I'M TOAST! BURNT TOAST!
CHUNK
THE OLD CLUB INFERNO! 666 DIXON STREET!
THAT'S IT! THAT'S ALL I GOT! HONEST!
DON'T WORRY, EEL. WHEN I NEED TO KNOW MORE, I KNOW WHERE TO FIND YOU.
TELL ME SOMETHIN' I DON'T KNOW, YA PUTRID PUNK!
VRMMM

I DON'T GET IT, BOSS. WHY DID YOU PUMP EEL FOR INFORMATION... ...THAT YOU ALREADY *KNEW* AS MATCHES MALONE?

BECAUSE EEL DOESN'T *KNOW* THAT I KNOW.

OKAY, "JOEY"...

...BUT YOU CAN'T TELL CHANDLER AND MONICA.

WHAT?

SORRY, POP CULTURE REFERENCE. SAY...

...I NOTICED ONE OF THE "SPECIAL" SUITS HAS BEEN CHECKED OUT FROM THE BATCAVE. THE *FIREPROOF ARMOR.*

EXPECTING SOME OF FIREFLY'S EXPLOSIVE LITTLE SURPRISES?

CLUB INFERNO

CLUB INFERNO

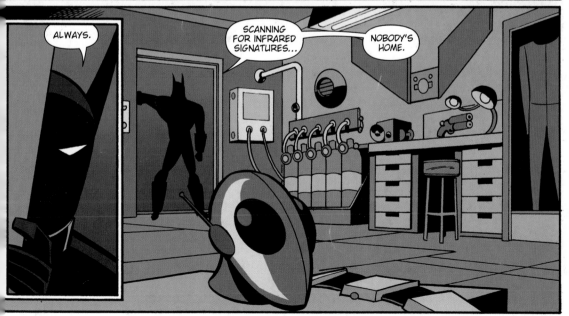

ALWAYS.

SCANNING FOR INFRARED SIGNATURES...

NOBODY'S HOME.

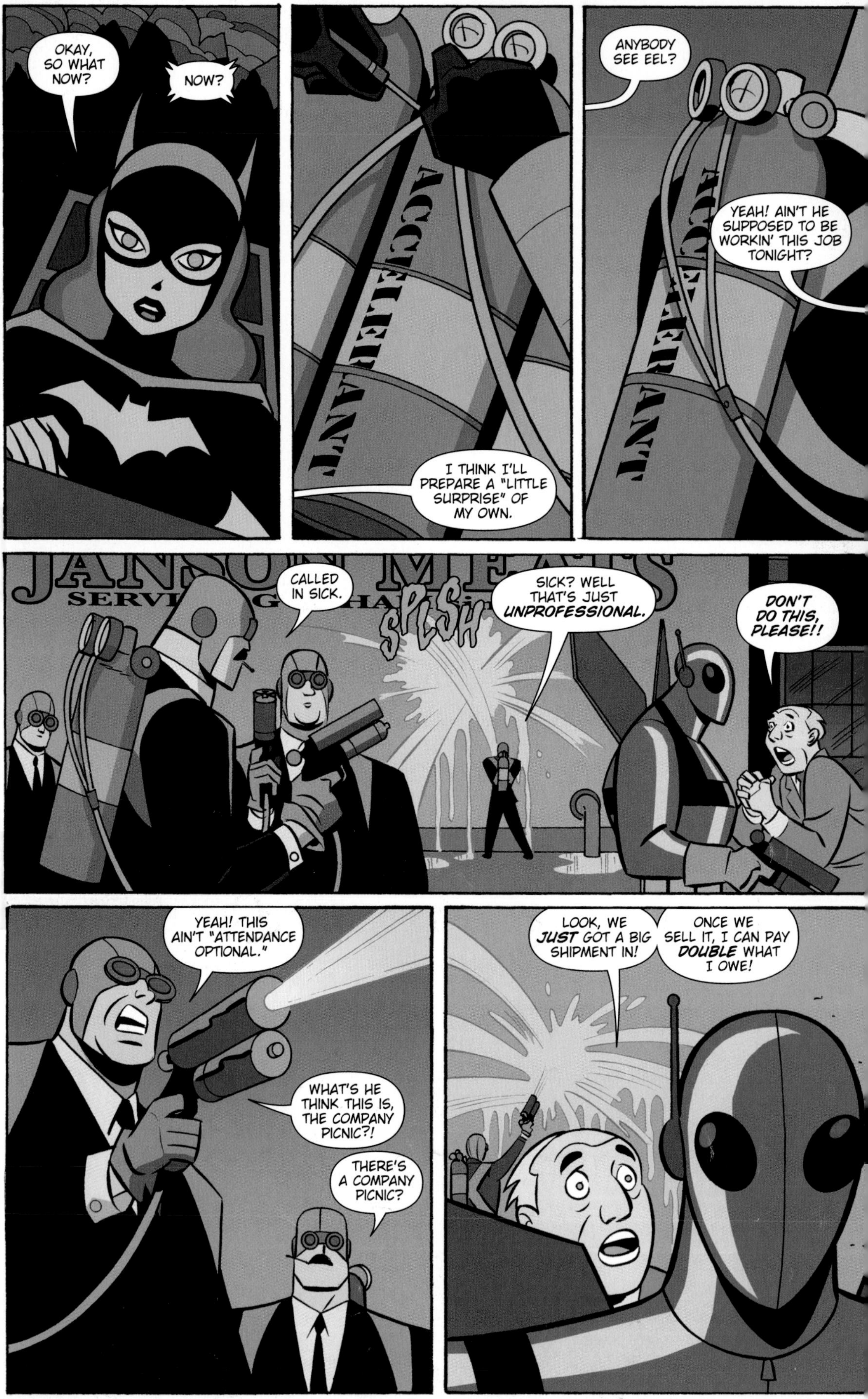
OKAY, SO WHAT NOW?
NOW?
I THINK I'LL PREPARE A "LITTLE SURPRISE" OF MY OWN.
ACCELERANT
ANYBODY SEE EEL?
YEAH! AIN'T HE SUPPOSED TO BE WORKIN' THIS JOB TONIGHT?
CALLED IN SICK.
SPLSH
SICK? WELL THAT'S JUST UNPROFESSIONAL.
DON'T DO THIS, PLEASE!!
YEAH! THIS AIN'T "ATTENDANCE OPTIONAL."
WHAT'S HE THINK THIS IS, THE COMPANY PICNIC?!
THERE'S A COMPANY PICNIC?
LOOK, WE JUST GOT A BIG SHIPMENT IN!
ONCE WE SELL IT, I CAN PAY DOUBLE WHAT I OWE!

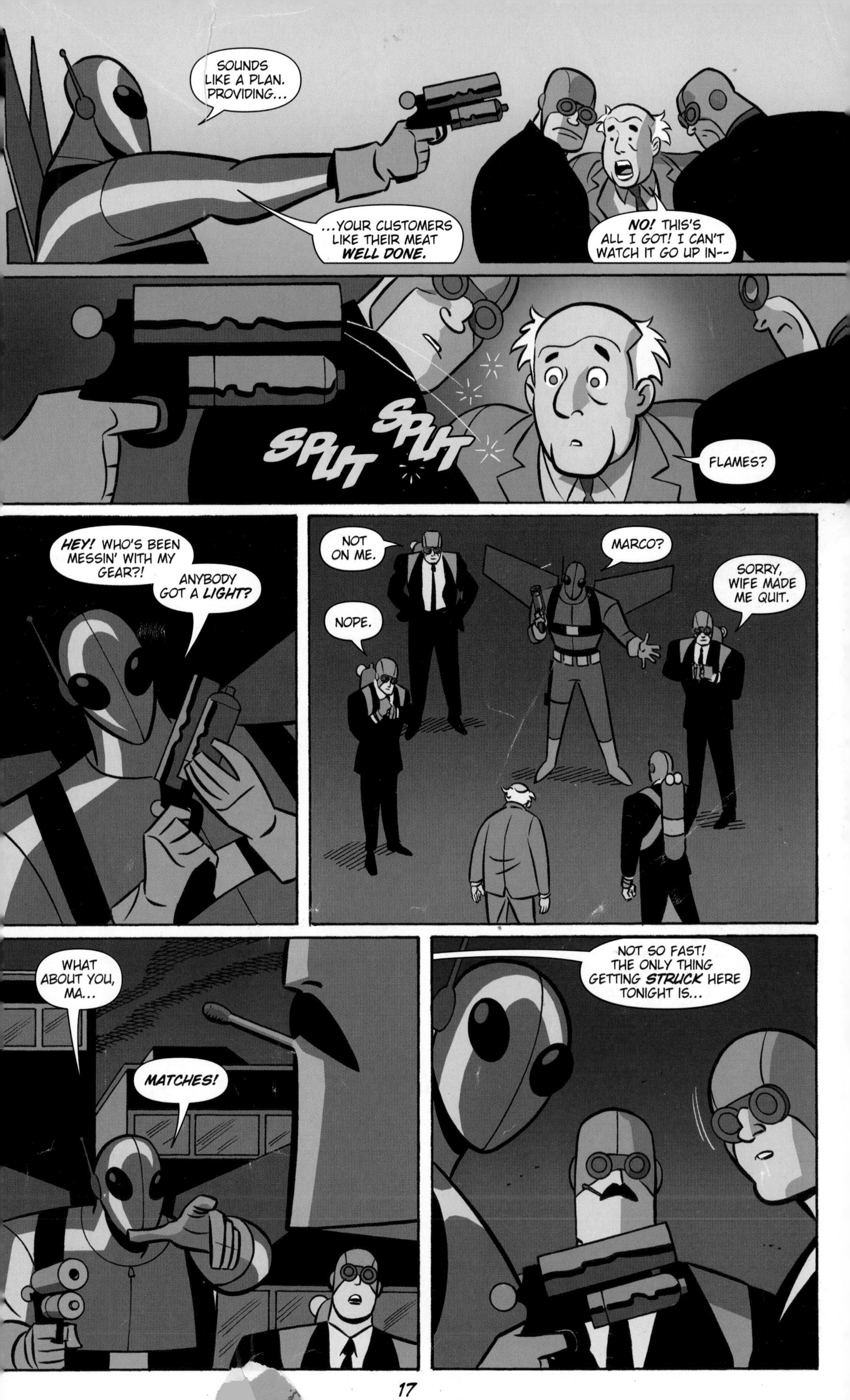

SOUNDS LIKE A PLAN. PROVIDING...
...YOUR CUSTOMERS LIKE THEIR MEAT **WELL DONE.**
NO! THIS'S ALL I GOT! I CAN'T WATCH IT GO UP IN--
SPUT SPUT
FLAMES?
HEY! WHO'S BEEN MESSIN' WITH MY GEAR?!
ANYBODY GOT A **LIGHT?**
NOT ON ME.
NOPE.
MARCO?
SORRY, WIFE MADE ME QUIT.
WHAT ABOUT YOU, MA...
MATCHES!
NOT SO FAST! THE ONLY THING GETTING **STRUCK** HERE TONIGHT IS...

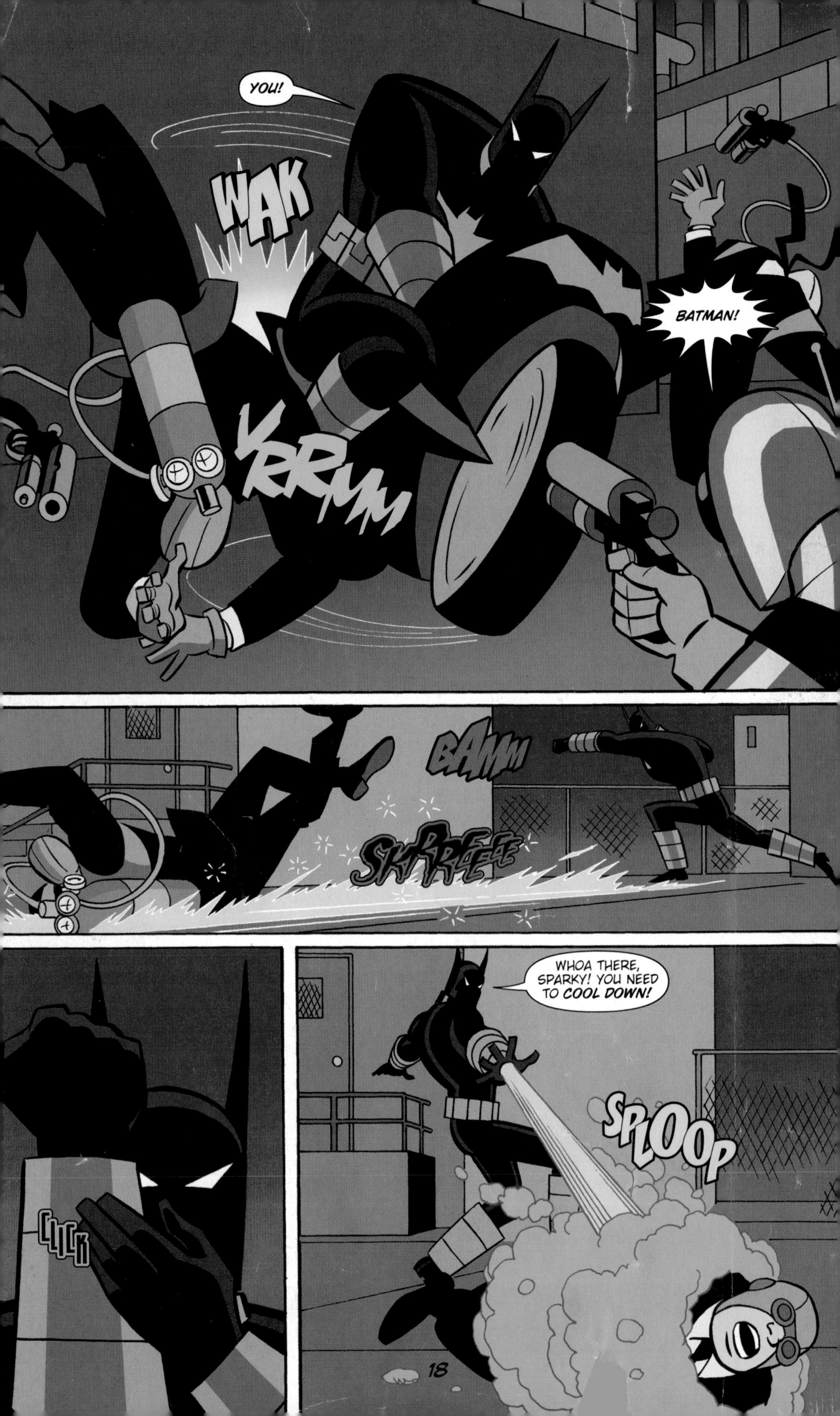
YOU!
WAK
BATMAN!
VRRMM
BAMM
SKRREEE
WHOA THERE, SPARKY! YOU NEED TO COOL DOWN!
SPLOOP
CLICK

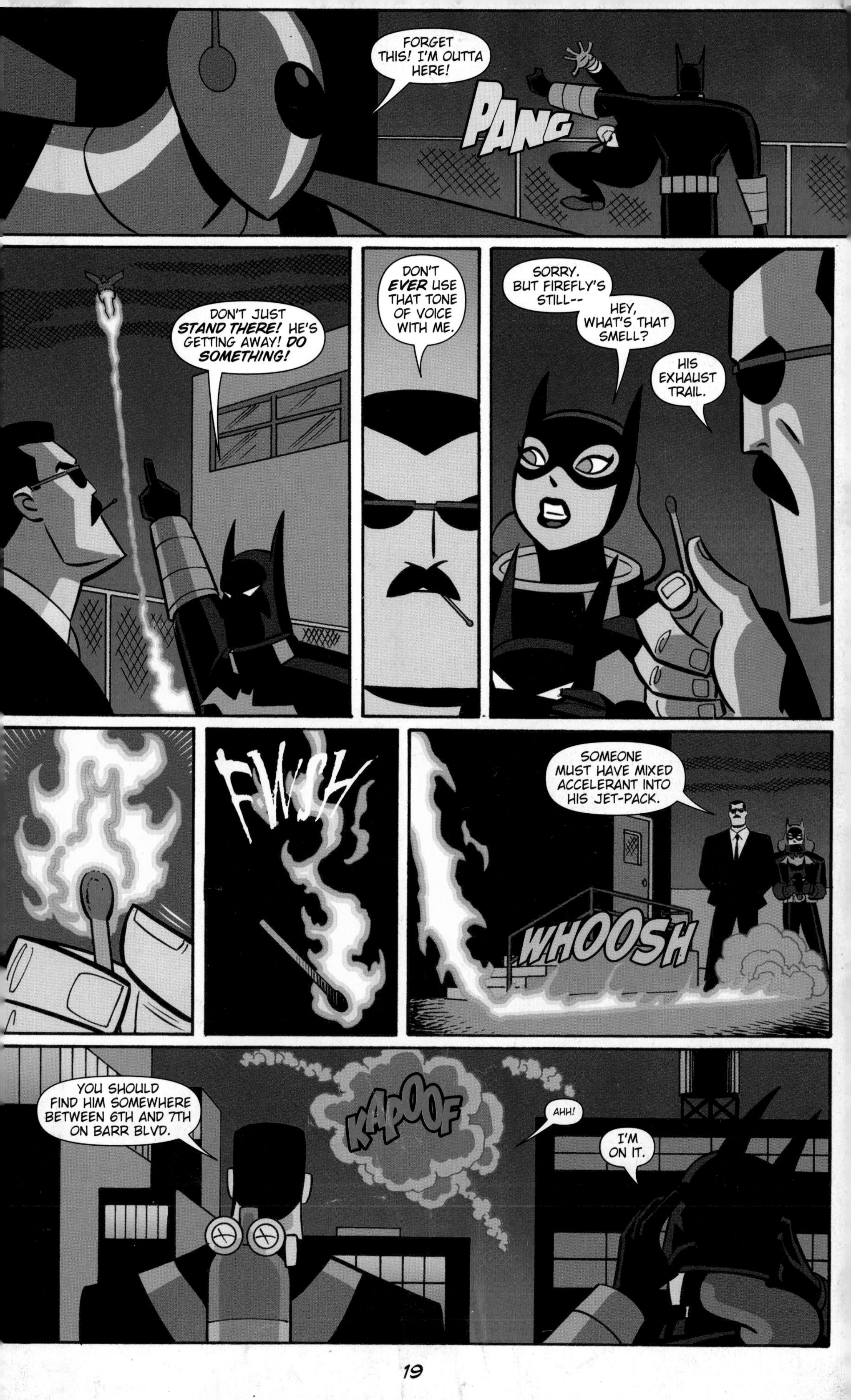
FORGET THIS! I'M OUTTA HERE!
PANG
DON'T JUST STAND THERE! HE'S GETTING AWAY! DO SOMETHING!
DON'T EVER USE THAT TONE OF VOICE WITH ME.
SORRY. BUT FIREFLY'S STILL--
HEY, WHAT'S THAT SMELL?
HIS EXHAUST TRAIL.
FWSH
SOMEONE MUST HAVE MIXED ACCELERANT INTO HIS JET-PACK.
WHOOSH
YOU SHOULD FIND HIM SOMEWHERE BETWEEN 6TH AND 7TH ON BARR BLVD.
KAPOOF
AHH!
I'M ON IT.

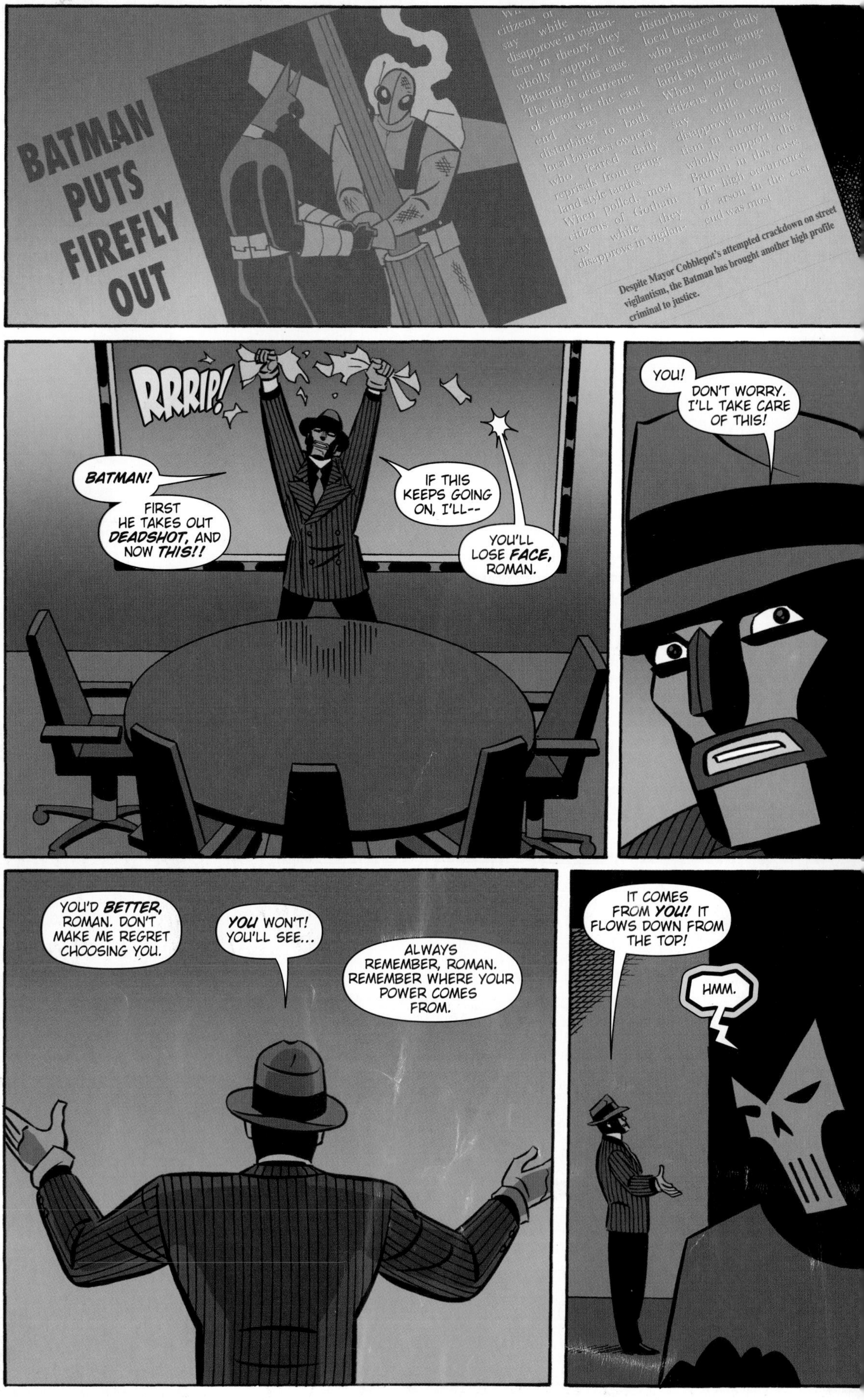
BATMAN PUTS FIREFLY OUT
Despite Mayor Cobblepot's attempted crackdown on street vigilantism, the Batman has brought another high profile criminal to justice.
RRRIP!
BATMAN!
FIRST HE TAKES OUT DEADSHOT, AND NOW THIS!!
IF THIS KEEPS GOING ON, I'LL--
YOU'LL LOSE FACE, ROMAN.
YOU!
DON'T WORRY. I'LL TAKE CARE OF THIS!
YOU'D BETTER, ROMAN. DON'T MAKE ME REGRET CHOOSING YOU.
YOU WON'T! YOU'LL SEE...
ALWAYS REMEMBER, ROMAN. REMEMBER WHERE YOUR POWER COMES FROM.
IT COMES FROM YOU! IT FLOWS DOWN FROM THE TOP!
HMM.

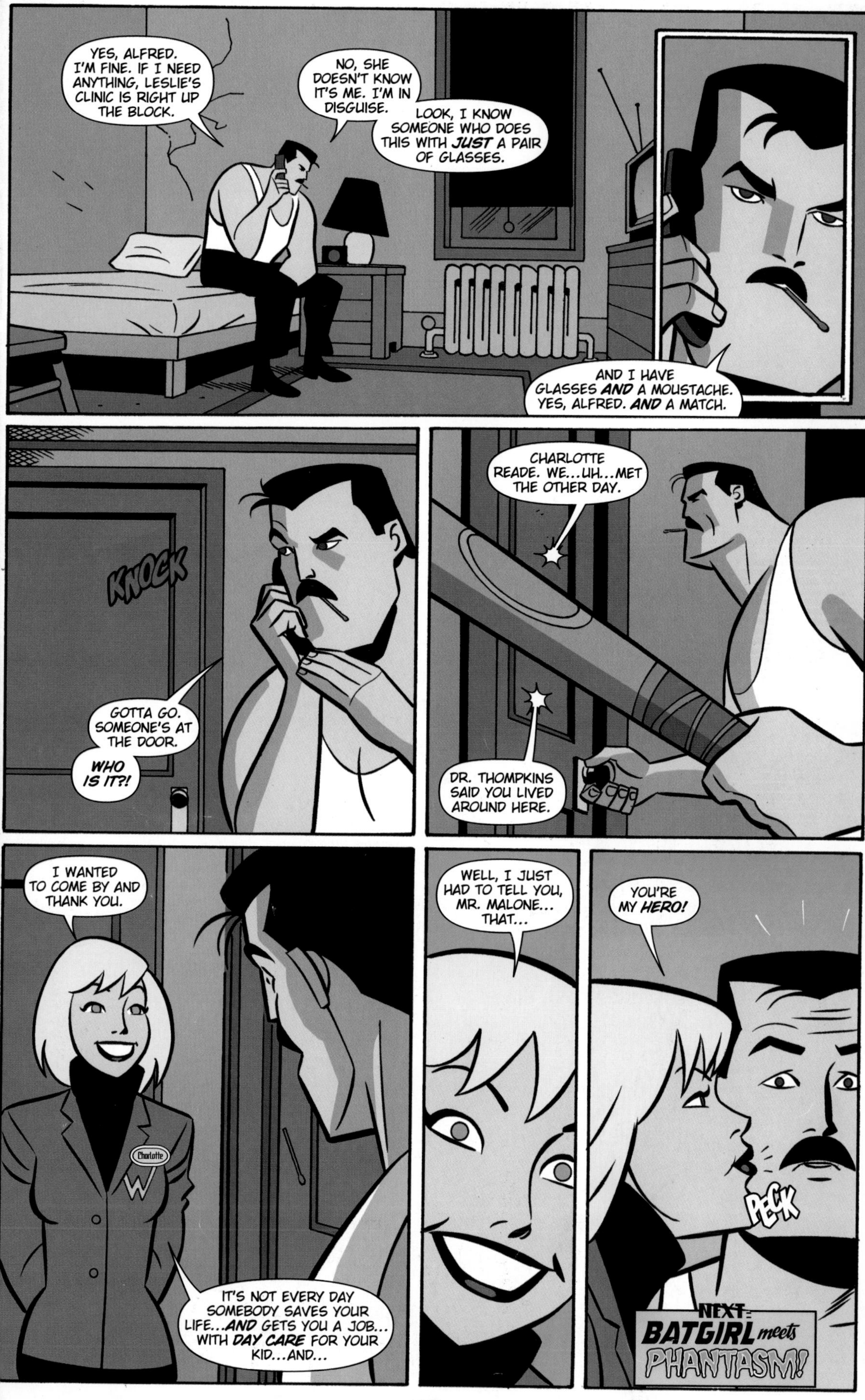
YES, ALFRED. I'M FINE. IF I NEED ANYTHING, LESLIE'S CLINIC IS RIGHT UP THE BLOCK.
NO, SHE DOESN'T KNOW IT'S ME. I'M IN DISGUISE.
LOOK, I KNOW SOMEONE WHO DOES THIS WITH *JUST* A PAIR OF GLASSES.
AND I HAVE GLASSES *AND* A MOUSTACHE. YES, ALFRED. *AND* A MATCH.
KNOCK
GOTTA GO. SOMEONE'S AT THE DOOR.
WHO IS IT?!
CHARLOTTE READE. WE...UH...MET THE OTHER DAY.
DR. THOMPKINS SAID YOU LIVED AROUND HERE.
I WANTED TO COME BY AND THANK YOU.
Charlotte
IT'S NOT EVERY DAY SOMEBODY SAVES YOUR LIFE...*AND* GETS YOU A JOB... WITH *DAY CARE* FOR YOUR KID...AND...
WELL, I JUST HAD TO TELL YOU, MR. MALONE... THAT...
YOU'RE MY *HERO!*
PECK
NEXT: BATGIRL meets PHANTASM!

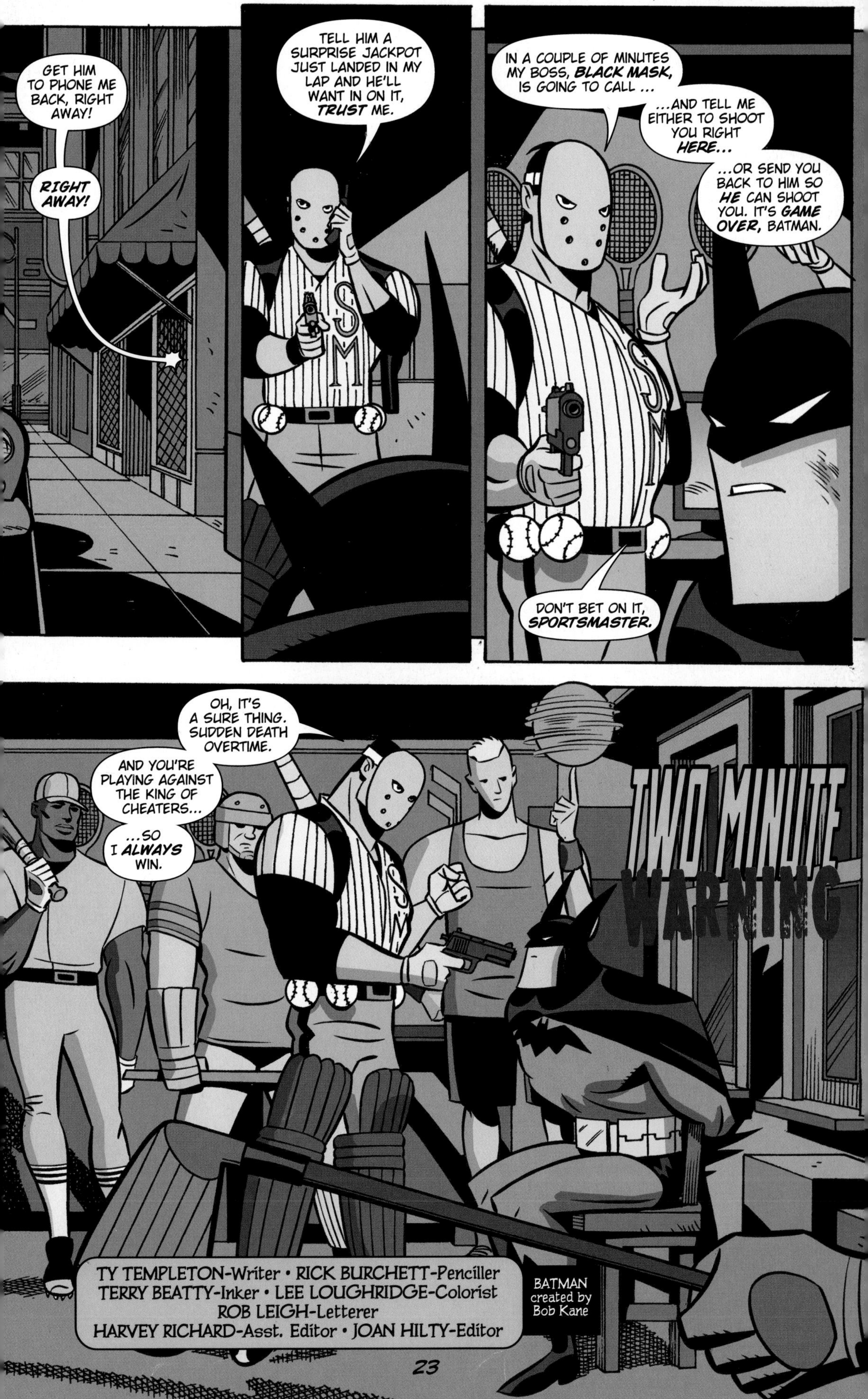

GET HIM TO PHONE ME BACK, RIGHT AWAY!
RIGHT AWAY!
TELL HIM A SURPRISE JACKPOT JUST LANDED IN MY LAP AND HE'LL WANT IN ON IT, TRUST ME.
IN A COUPLE OF MINUTES MY BOSS, BLACK MASK, IS GOING TO CALL ...
...AND TELL ME EITHER TO SHOOT YOU RIGHT HERE...
...OR SEND YOU BACK TO HIM SO HE CAN SHOOT YOU. IT'S GAME OVER, BATMAN.
DON'T BET ON IT, SPORTSMASTER.
OH, IT'S A SURE THING. SUDDEN DEATH OVERTIME.
AND YOU'RE PLAYING AGAINST THE KING OF CHEATERS...
...SO I ALWAYS WIN.
TWO MINUTE WARNING
TY TEMPLETON-Writer • RICK BURCHETT-Penciller
TERRY BEATTY-Inker • LEE LOUGHRIDGE-Colorist
ROB LEIGH-Letterer
HARVEY RICHARD-Asst. Editor • JOAN HILTY-Editor
BATMAN created by Bob Kane

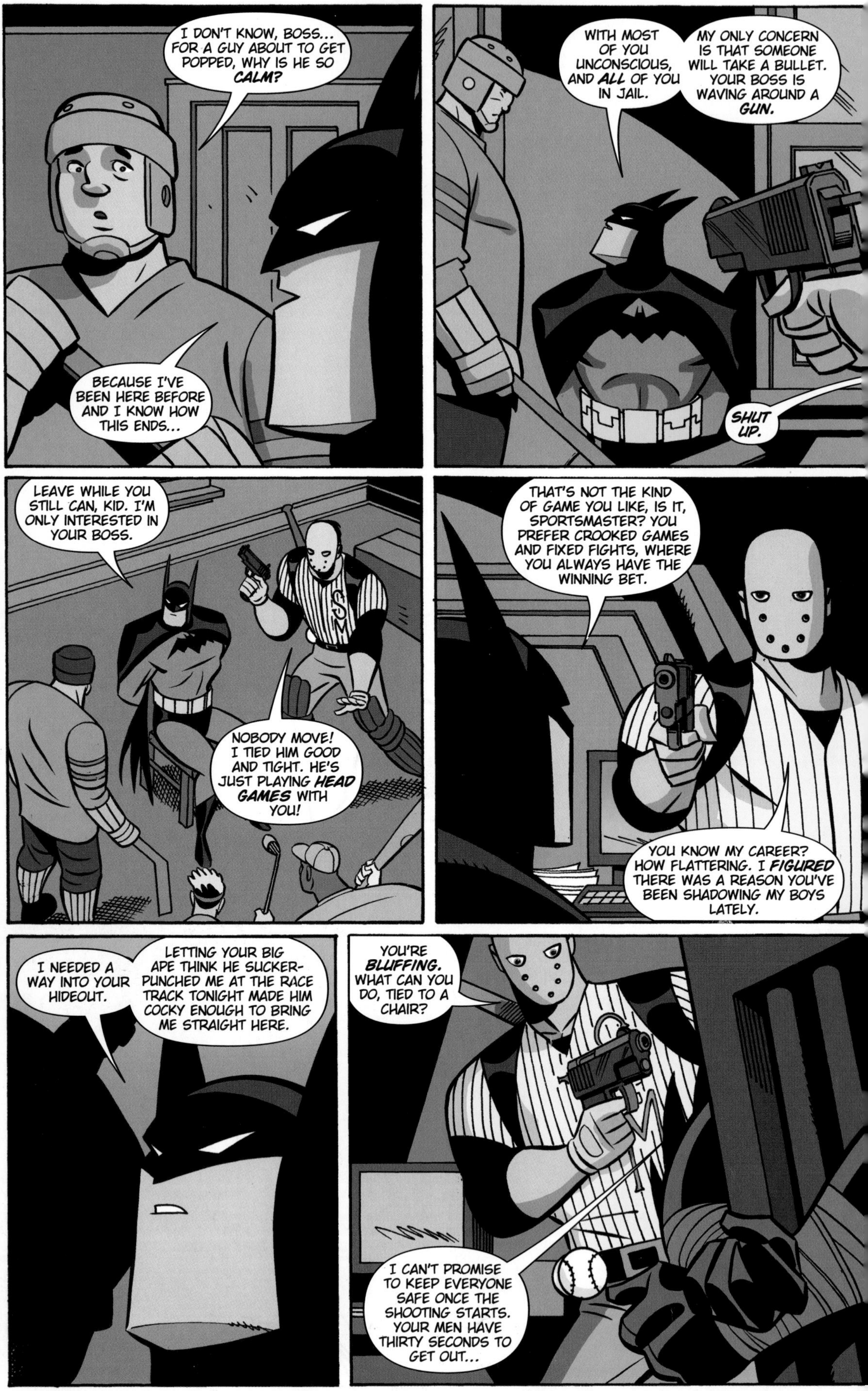

I DON'T KNOW, BOSS... FOR A GUY ABOUT TO GET POPPED, WHY IS HE SO CALM?
BECAUSE I'VE BEEN HERE BEFORE AND I KNOW HOW THIS ENDS...
WITH MOST OF YOU UNCONSCIOUS, AND ALL OF YOU IN JAIL.
MY ONLY CONCERN IS THAT SOMEONE WILL TAKE A BULLET. YOUR BOSS IS WAVING AROUND A GUN.
SHUT UP.
LEAVE WHILE YOU STILL CAN, KID. I'M ONLY INTERESTED IN YOUR BOSS.
NOBODY MOVE! I TIED HIM GOOD AND TIGHT. HE'S JUST PLAYING HEAD GAMES WITH YOU!
THAT'S NOT THE KIND OF GAME YOU LIKE, IS IT, SPORTSMASTER? YOU PREFER CROOKED GAMES AND FIXED FIGHTS, WHERE YOU ALWAYS HAVE THE WINNING BET.
YOU KNOW MY CAREER? HOW FLATTERING. I FIGURED THERE WAS A REASON YOU'VE BEEN SHADOWING MY BOYS LATELY.
I NEEDED A WAY INTO YOUR HIDEOUT.
LETTING YOUR BIG APE THINK HE SUCKER-PUNCHED ME AT THE RACE TRACK TONIGHT MADE HIM COCKY ENOUGH TO BRING ME STRAIGHT HERE.
YOU'RE BLUFFING. WHAT CAN YOU DO, TIED TO A CHAIR?
I CAN'T PROMISE TO KEEP EVERYONE SAFE ONCE THE SHOOTING STARTS. YOUR MEN HAVE THIRTY SECONDS TO GET OUT...

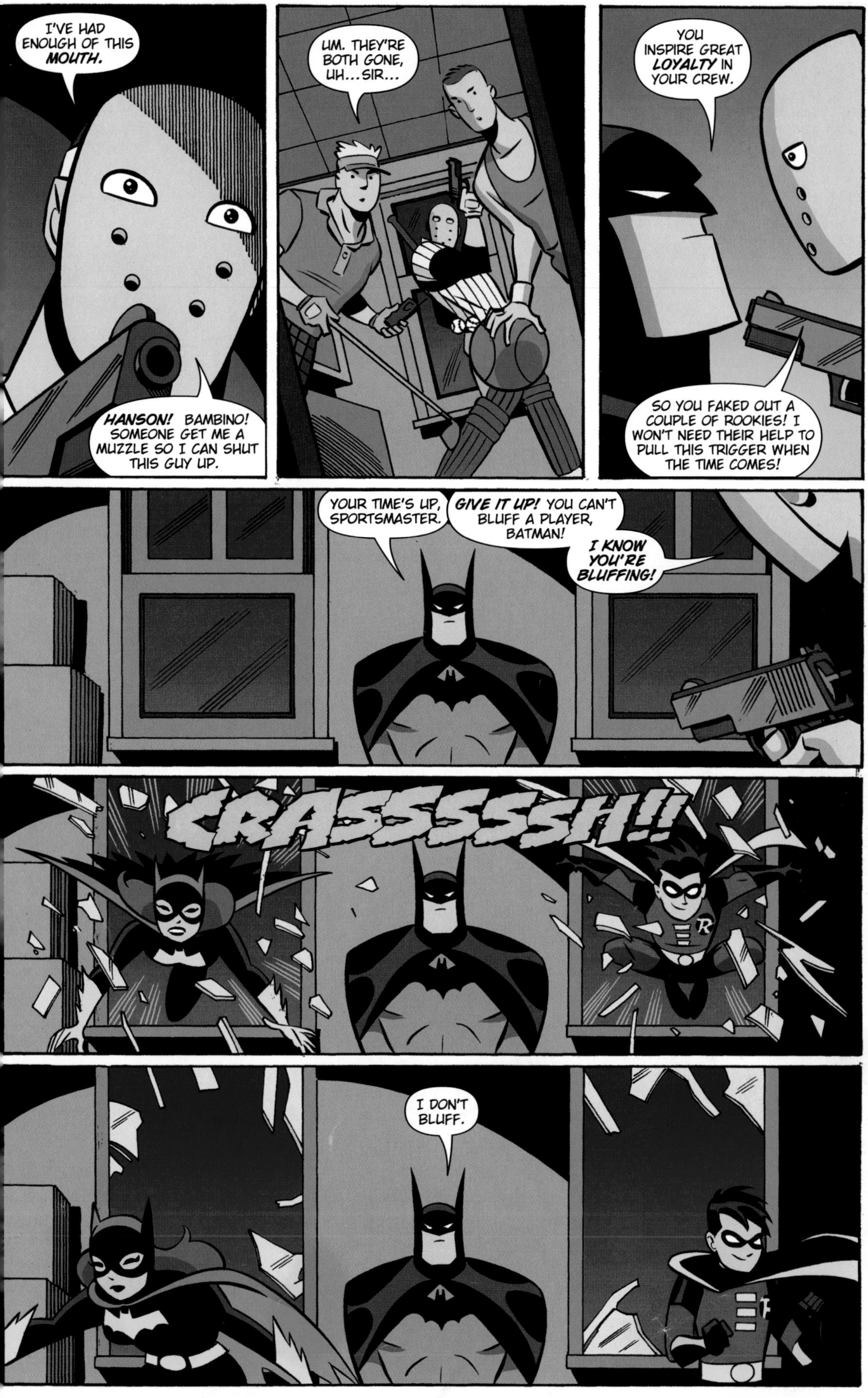
I'VE HAD ENOUGH OF THIS *MOUTH.*
HANSON! BAMBINO! SOMEONE GET ME A MUZZLE SO I CAN SHUT THIS GUY UP.
UM. THEY'RE BOTH GONE, UH... SIR...
YOU INSPIRE GREAT *LOYALTY* IN YOUR CREW.
SO YOU FAKED OUT A COUPLE OF ROOKIES! I WON'T NEED THEIR HELP TO PULL THIS TRIGGER WHEN THE TIME COMES!
YOUR TIME'S UP, SPORTSMASTER.
GIVE IT UP! YOU CAN'T BLUFF A PLAYER, BATMAN!
I KNOW YOU'RE BLUFFING!
CRASSSSSH!!
I DON'T BLUFF.

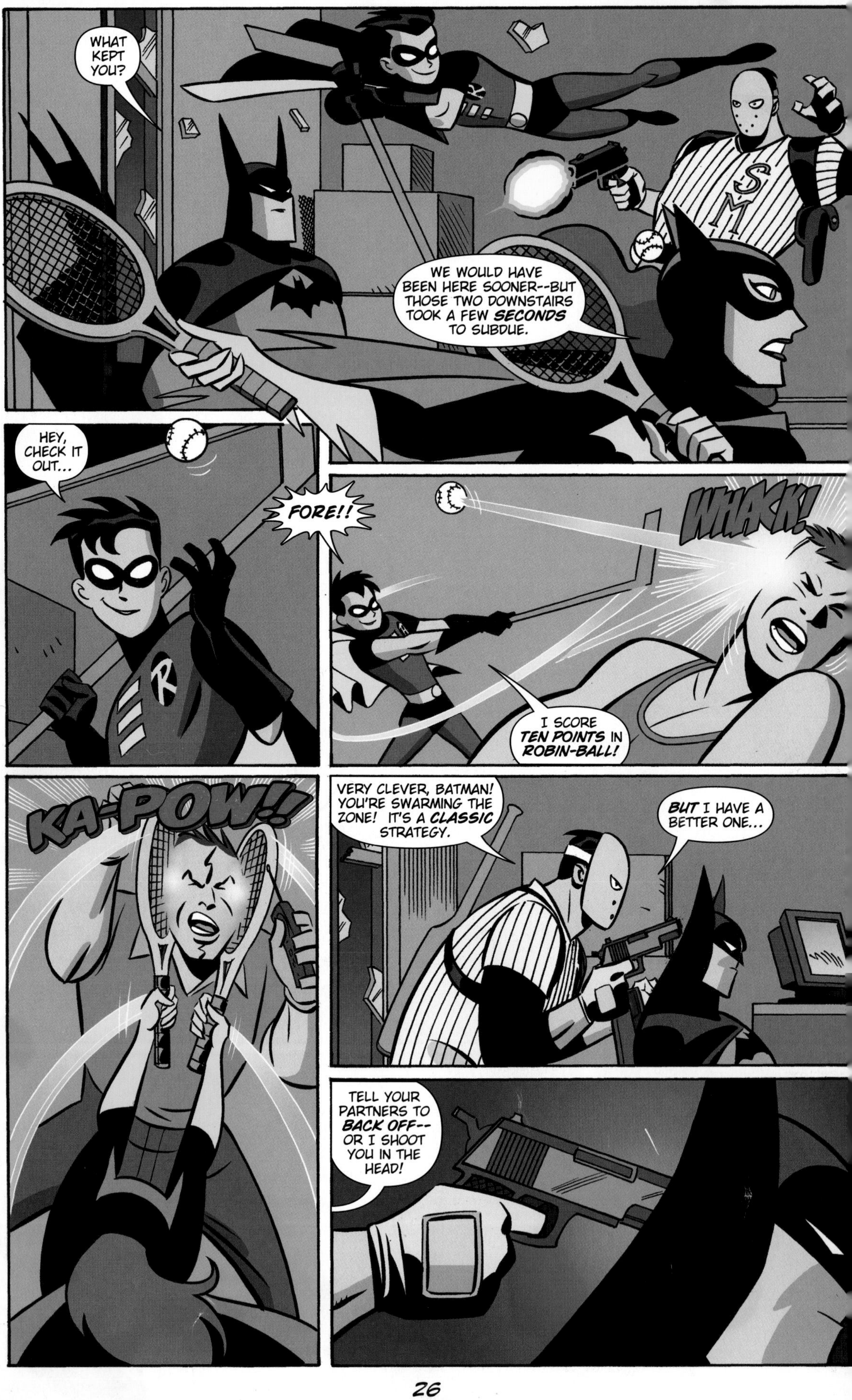
WHAT KEPT YOU?
WE WOULD HAVE BEEN HERE SOONER--BUT THOSE TWO DOWNSTAIRS TOOK A FEW SECONDS TO SUBDUE.
HEY, CHECK IT OUT...
FORE!!
WHACK!
I SCORE TEN POINTS IN ROBIN-BALL!
KA-POW!!
VERY CLEVER, BATMAN! YOU'RE SWARMING THE ZONE! IT'S A CLASSIC STRATEGY.
BUT I HAVE A BETTER ONE...
TELL YOUR PARTNERS TO BACK OFF--OR I SHOOT YOU IN THE HEAD!

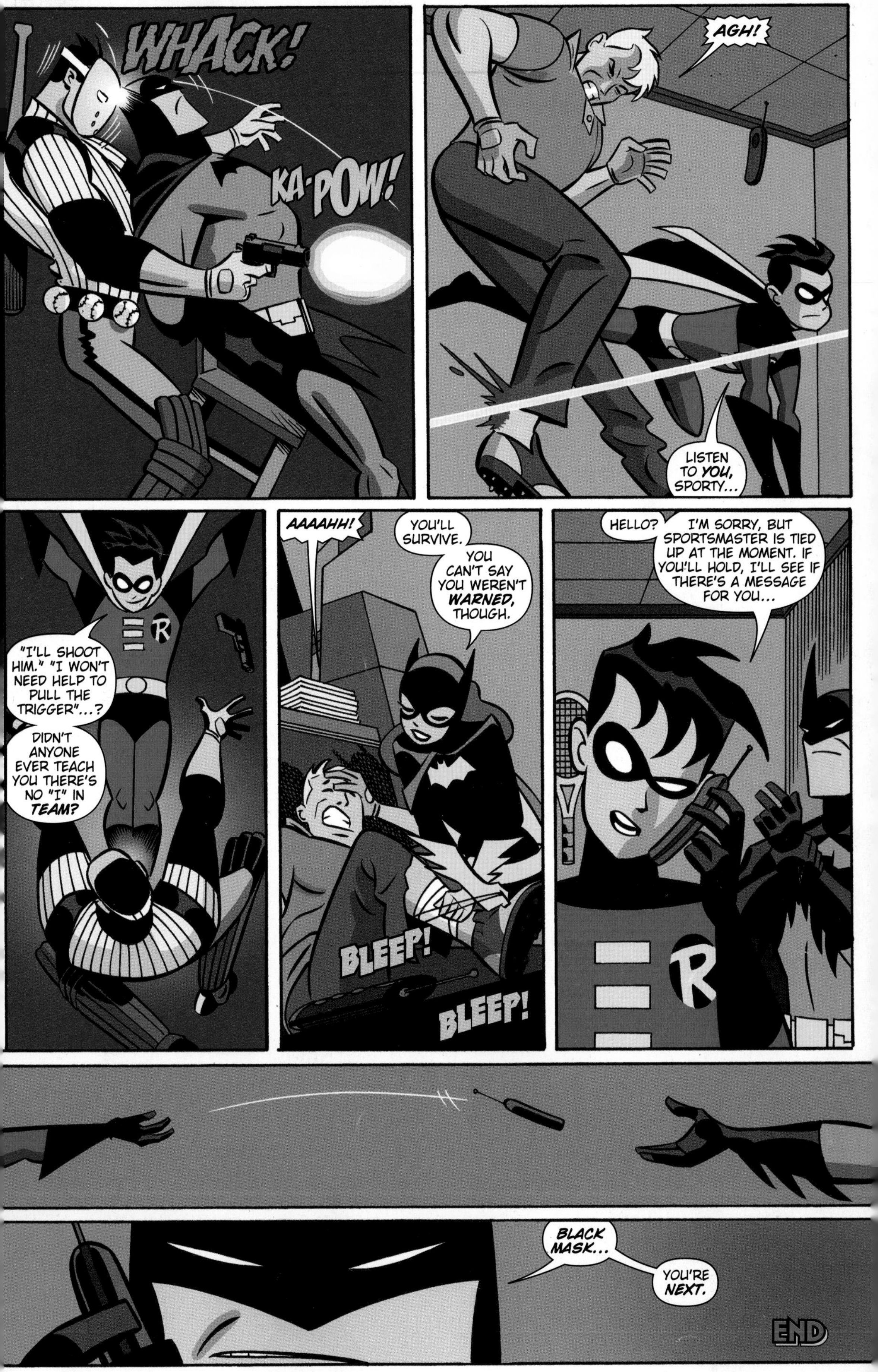

WHACK!
KA-POW!
AGH!
LISTEN TO YOU, SPORTY...
"I'LL SHOOT HIM." "I WON'T NEED HELP TO PULL THE TRIGGER"...?
DIDN'T ANYONE EVER TEACH YOU THERE'S NO "I" IN TEAM?
AAAAHH!
YOU'LL SURVIVE.
YOU CAN'T SAY YOU WEREN'T WARNED, THOUGH.
BLEEP!
BLEEP!
HELLO?
I'M SORRY, BUT SPORTSMASTER IS TIED UP AT THE MOMENT. IF YOU'LL HOLD, I'LL SEE IF THERE'S A MESSAGE FOR YOU...
BLACK MASK...
YOU'RE NEXT.
END

CREATORS

DAN SLOTT WRITER

Dan Slott is a comics writer best known for his work on DC Comics' Arkham Asylum, and, for Marvel, The Avengers and the Amazing Spider-Man.

RICK BURCHETT PENCILLER

Rick Burchett has worked as a comics artist for more than 25 years. He has received the comics industry's Eisner Award three times, Spain's Haxtur Award, and he has been nominated for the Eagle Award. Rick lives with his wife and two sons in Missouri, USA.

TERRY BEATTY INKER

For more than ten years, Terry Beatty was the main inker of DC Comics' "animated-style" Batman comics, including The Batman Strikes. More recently, he worked on *Return to Perdition*, a graphic novel for DC's Vertigo Crime.

LEE LOUGHRIDGE COLORIST

Lee Loughridge has been working in comics for more than fifteen years. He currently lives in sunny California in a tent on the beach.

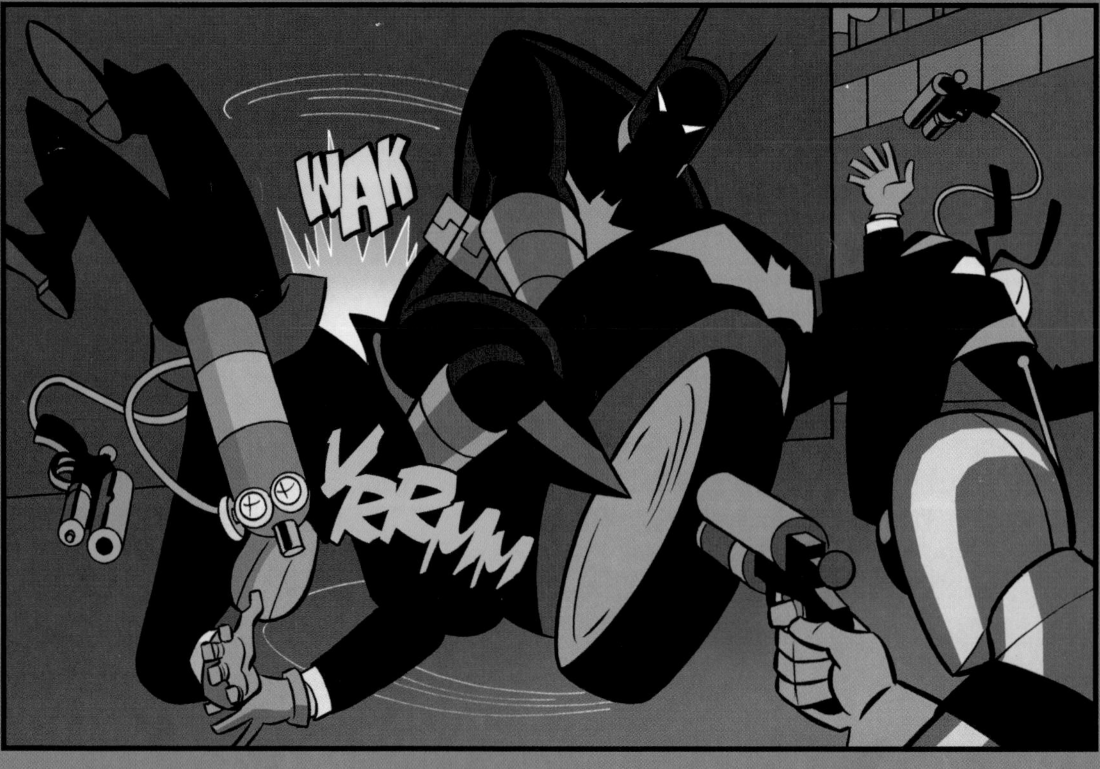
WAK
VRRMM

GLOSSARY

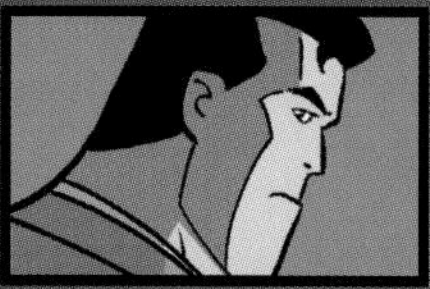
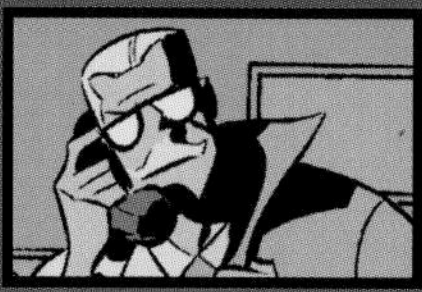
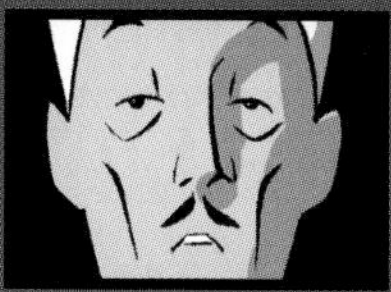

accelerant (ak-SEL-er-uhnt)--a substance that accelerates the spread of fire or makes a fire more intense

accessory (ak-SESS-uh-ree)--an accessory to a crime is someone who helps another person commit a crime or helps cover up a crime

arson (AR-suhn)--the deliberate act of setting fire to something

bluff (BLUHFF)--to pretend to be in a stronger position than you really are or to know more about something than you really do

exhaust (eg-ZAWST)--the waste gases produced by an engine

flattering (FLAT-ur-ing)--praising someone too much or insincerely, especially when you want a favor

inferno (in-FER-noh)--a flame-filled and extremely hot environment

perish (PAIR-ish)--to die, or to be destroyed

putrid (PYOO-trid)--rotten or evil

racketeering (rak-i-TEER-ing)--the practice of conducting or engaging in blackmail or bootlegging

subdue (suhb-DOO)--control or defeat

BATMAN GLOSSARY

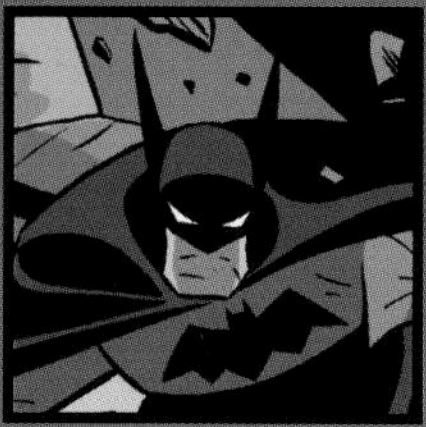
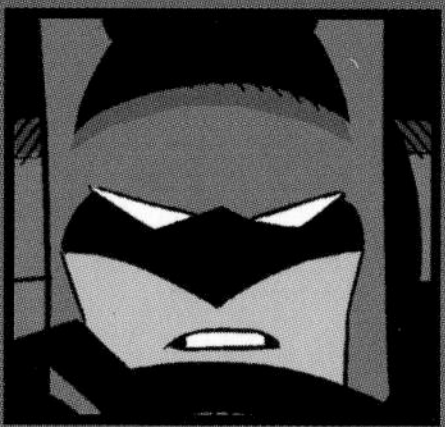
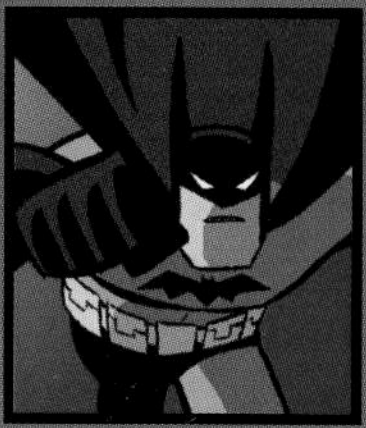

Alfred Pennyworth: Bruce Wayne's loyal butler. He knows Bruce Wayne's secret identity and helps the Dark Knight solve crimes in Gotham City.

Batgirl: Barbara Gordon, a.k.a. Batgirl, is one of Batman's most trusted crimefighting partners.

Black Mask: also known as Roman Sionis, Black Mask is a ruthless businessman and criminal boss of the Gotham underworld.

False Face Society: an organization of masked criminals who work for Black Mask. Each member of the Society chooses a mask to wear to disguise their true identity.

Firefly: a pyromaniac villain who wears a fireproof suit and wields a powerful flame thrower.

Matches Malone: a two-bit gangster Batman poses as to infiltrate criminal organizations.

Phantasm: despite posing as a man, Phantasm is actually Andrea Beaumont, a deadly martial artist who wields her scythe with expert skill.

Sportsmaster: a frustrated former athlete who turned to a life of crime.

VISUAL QUESTIONS & PROMPTS

1. Batgirl asked Batman why he interrogated Eel for information he already knew. Why was it important that Batman get the information despite already learning it as Matches Malone?

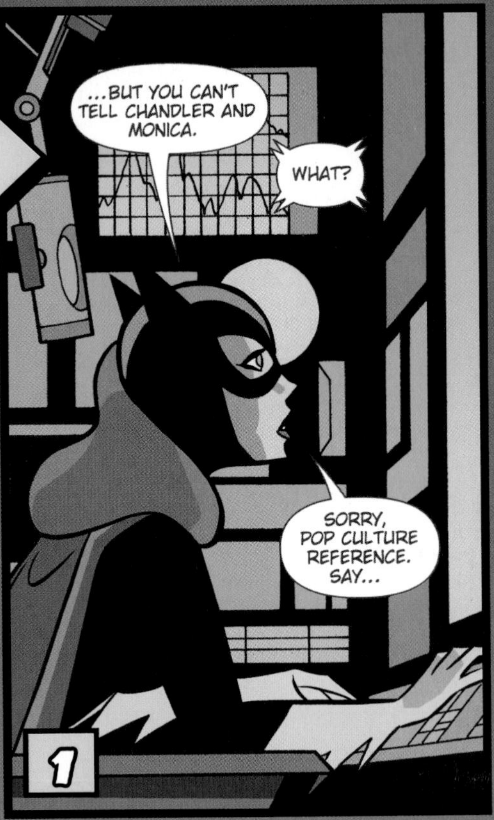
...BUT YOU CAN'T TELL CHANDLER AND MONICA.
WHAT?
SORRY, POP CULTURE REFERENCE. SAY...
1

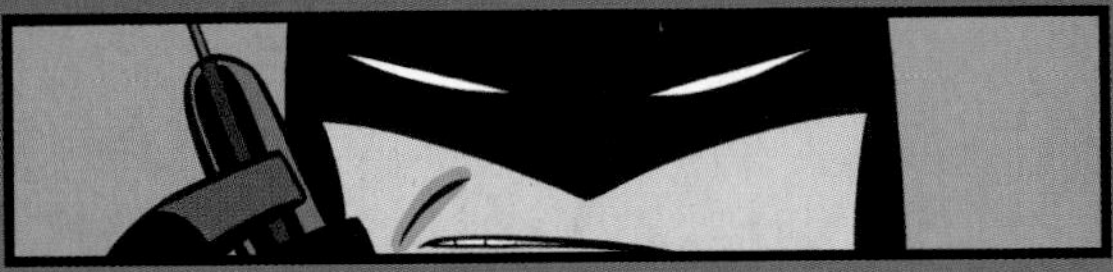

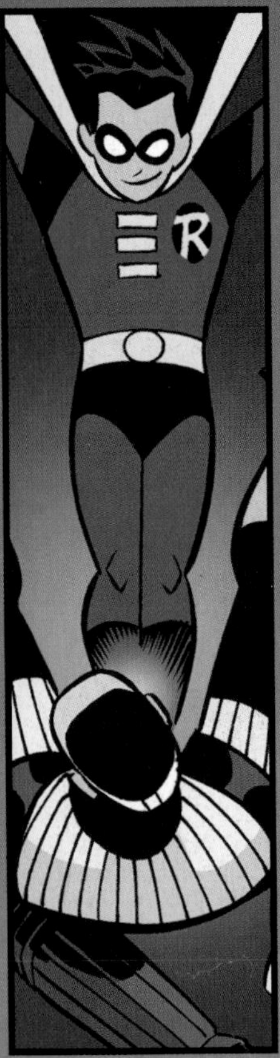

2. Why did the creators of this comic use a jagged panel border between these two panels?

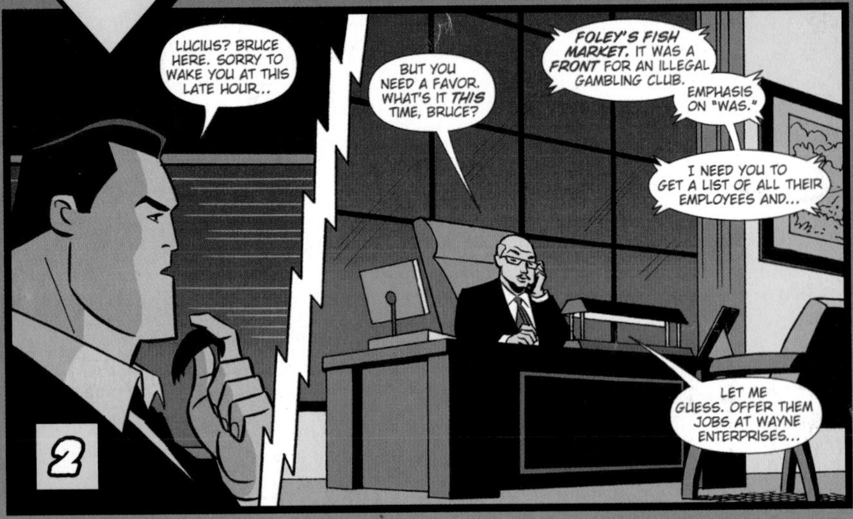
LUCIUS? BRUCE HERE. SORRY TO WAKE YOU AT THIS LATE HOUR...
BUT YOU NEED A FAVOR. WHAT'S IT *THIS* TIME, BRUCE?
FOLEY'S FISH MARKET. IT WAS A *FRONT* FOR AN ILLEGAL GAMBLING CLUB.
EMPHASIS ON "WAS."
I NEED YOU TO GET A LIST OF ALL THEIR EMPLOYEES AND...
LET ME GUESS. OFFER THEM JOBS AT WAYNE ENTERPRISES...
2

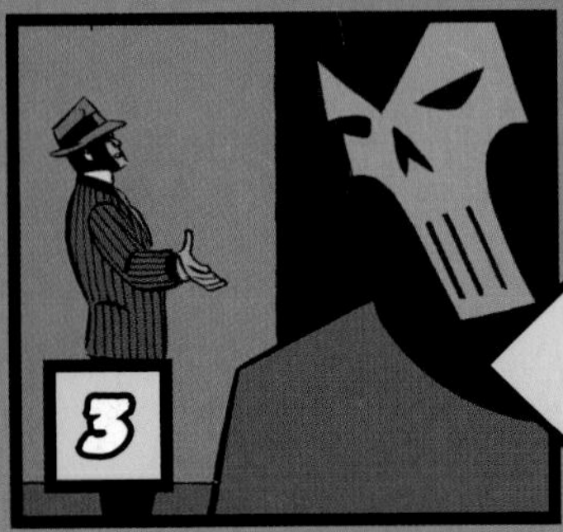
3

3. Based on the series of panels on page 20, who do you think is really in charge of the criminal organization - Black Mask or Andrea Beaumont, a.k.a. Phantasm? Why?

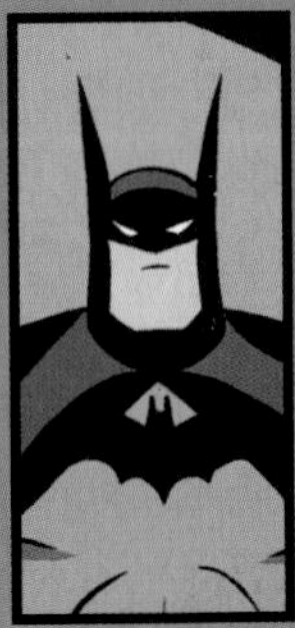

4. Who do you think Batman was epecting to be knocking on his door? Why would he be cautious of visitors?

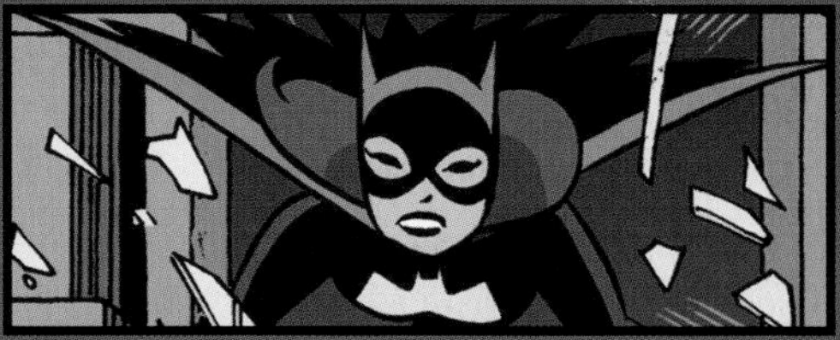

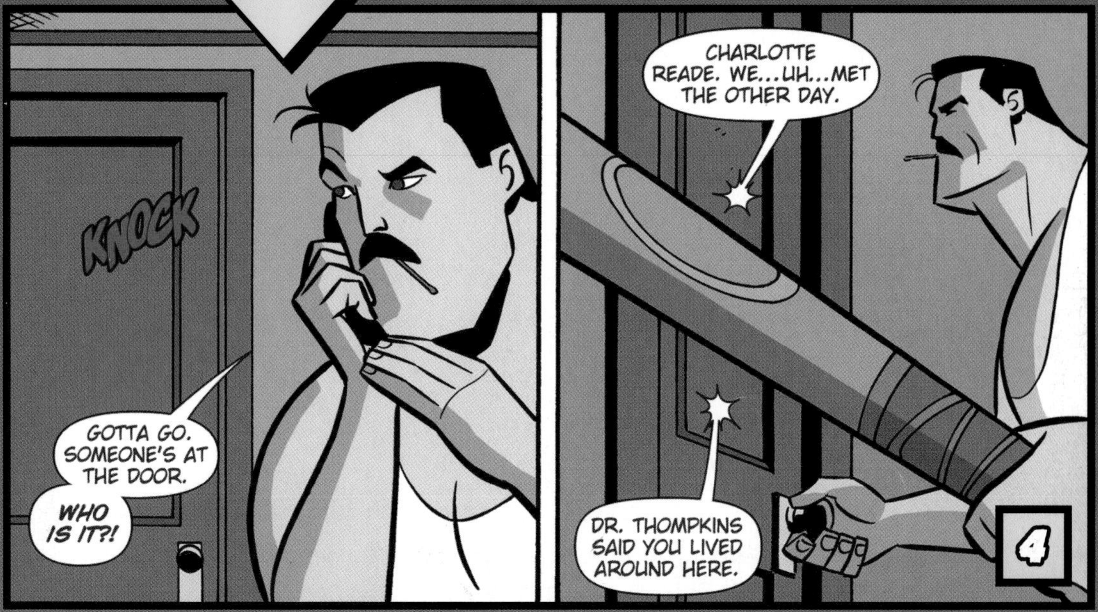
KNOCK
GOTTA GO. SOMEONE'S AT THE DOOR.
WHO IS IT?!
CHARLOTTE READE. WE...UH...MET THE OTHER DAY.
DR. THOMPKINS SAID YOU LIVED AROUND HERE.
4

5. At what point in this story did you realize that Batgirl was posing as Batman? What clues gave it away?

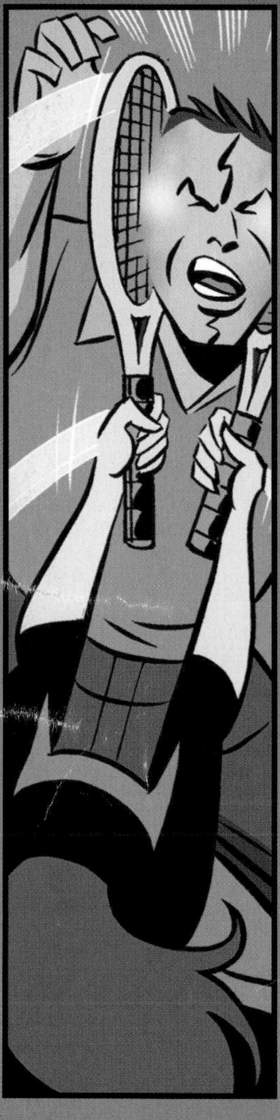

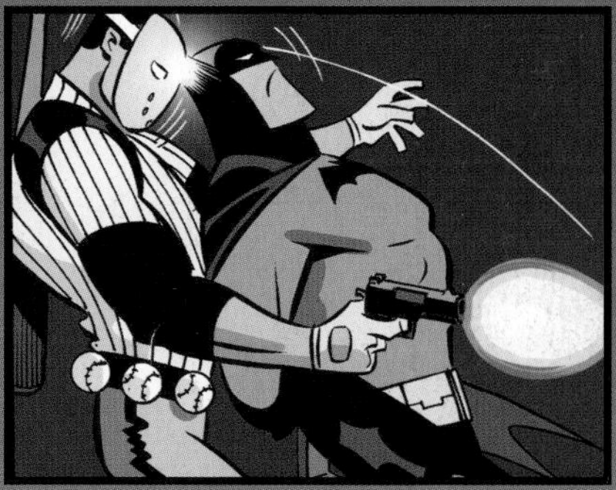

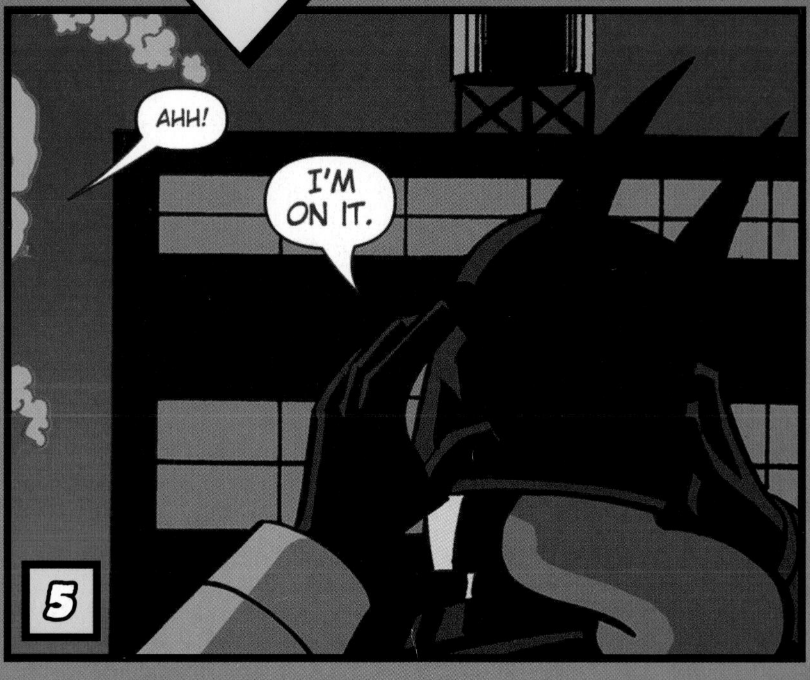
AHH!
I'M ON IT.
5

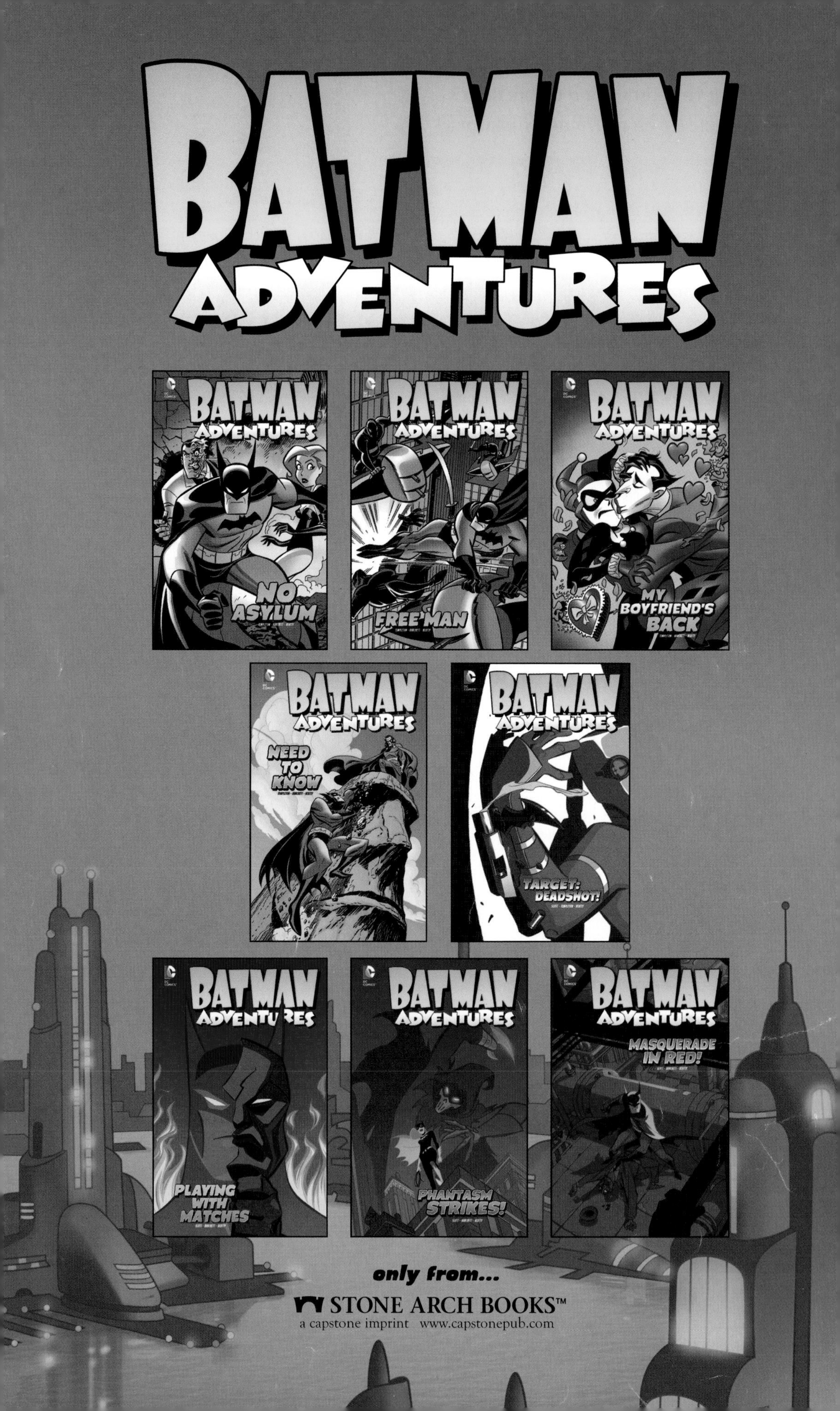
BATMAN ADVENTURES
BATMAN ADVENTURES
NO ASYLUM
BATMAN ADVENTURES
FREE MAN
BATMAN ADVENTURES
MY BOYFRIEND'S BACK
BATMAN ADVENTURES
NEED TO KNOW
BATMAN ADVENTURES
TARGET: DEADSHOT!
BATMAN ADVENTURES
PLAYING WITH MATCHES
BATMAN ADVENTURES
PHANTASM STRIKES!
BATMAN ADVENTURES
MASQUERADE IN RED!
only from...
STONE ARCH BOOKS™
a capstone imprint www.capstonepub.com